HIDEAWAY WILLOW

To Myrna my good friend
Marjorie Hands

HIDEAWAY WILLOW

by

Marjorie Hands

CENTRAL PUBLISHING SERVICES.
West Yorkshire

Paperback ISBN 1 903970 92 X

Produced
by

Central Publishing Services.
Royd Street Offices
Milnsbridge
Huddersfield
West Yorkshire
HD3 4QY

www.centralpublishing.co.uk

Hideaway Willow

Part 1

CHAPTER 1

Ten year old Sam stood outside the gate of number twelve, his eyes hard with anger, his mouth set in a tight line, his teeth clenched against the tears that threatened as he watched the two men in grey dustcoats carry out the furniture and dump it unceremoniously on the rough grass that passed for a lawn in front of the house. A little knot of neighbours stood watching too, murmuring their disapproval. "Shame!" he heard one say. "Scandalous!" "It's disgusting, that's what it is, turning the poor woman out like this, and her with a bairn too."

"Don't blame us, missus, we're only doing our job." the tall skinny man said, "It's not our fault if she didn't pay the rent."

Sam stood silent, his heart holding nothing but contempt for the women. He couldn't remember any one of them ever having a kind word for either him or his mother. The other man, the fat one, came out carrying a torn, stained mattress. Sam turned away, ashamed. That was his mattress. It was all Snowy's fault. She'd had her young ones on that mattress, scratching a hole in it to make a nest for the four tiny rabbits that blindly clung to her for their food. He knew his mother hadn't been pleased about the mess but she'd said nothing. She rarely did. He wondered what they had done with Snowy and her babies. Uncle Dave had said he couldn't take them with him. His protests had been brushed aside.

"No, Sam. Your Aunty Hilda won't have 'em. I'll see they're alright, lad. I promise I'll find a good home for 'em." and with that he'd had to be content. Nevertheless Snowy would have been something to hold on to in his misery. He could have told her his troubles as he usually did when things went wrong. Even so, he realised that Snowy was the least of his worries right now.

Sam leaned over the gate, alert and watchful as the two men brought out the chest of drawers from his bedroom. He had had no chance to rescue the secret hoard that he kept hidden under the top left-hand drawer - a collection of those little things a boy thinks might come in useful - penknife, pencil stubs, string and an empty cotton reel. As soon as the men disappeared back inside the house Sam was through the gate, giving only a brief disdainful glance at the watchers. He pulled out the drawer and slid his hand inside the opening. His fingers felt the smooth surface of the box that fitted so snugly at the back - the box that held his treasures. The fat man came through the front door at that moment and seeing Sam with his hand inside the chest of drawers, yelled at him. Sam made a grab for the box and turned to make his escape but the man was quick despite his bulk and caught Sam by the collar.

"Now then, what d'you think you're doing, eh? What have you got there you young devil? Give it to me."

"It's mine." Sam's voice was high with indignation.

"Give it to me," the man insisted.

"No."

"Leave him alone," one of the women shouted. "It does belong to him. He lives here."

"Did, you mean."

"Did you live here?"

Sam nodded, unable now to stem the tears that had threatened so long. He brushed them away with his sleeve, ashamed that he should cry in front of the neighbours.

"I'm sorry, lad." the man put out a podgy hand and ruffled Sam's hair. "I'm real sorry. Here," he took a note from his pocket, "get yourself some toffees, eh?"

Sam looked down at the note in his hand and his eyes goggled, Ten bob! What he couldn't do with ten bob! "Ta," he said, wiping his eyes and his nose on the sleeve of his jersey. "Ta, mister," and he fled before the man could change his mind and take the money back.

Sam's first stop was the newsagent's where he viewed the row of chocolate bars with a critical eye. He chose three of his favourites, deciding that he wasn't going to spend all the money at once. He'd save some, make it last, hide what was left so he wouldn't have to give any to Paul. After all Paul always got pocket money from his dad. Sam only managed to get a few coppers when his Mam was "flush". Anyway, there probably wouldn't be anything at all now. Not now his Mam wasn't there anymore. With his purchases tucked safely in his trouser pocket Sam made for the park. He slipped through the railings and headed for his secret den under the willow tree. It's branches, drooping down to the river on one side and to the grass on the other made it a perfect hideaway, a secret place, where no one could see him. It was the place where Sam came when he wanted to be alone, a place where he could think, where he could sort out his troubles and, as he reflected, he had plenty of those now. He should have been at school but yesterday's episode had shocked him more than he cared to show. He'd left his Uncle Dave's house that morning but school had been the last place he wanted to be. He needed time to think, time to ponder on this new and disturbing situation in which he found himself. It had been only last Tuesday when the first inkling of what was to come had hit him. Uncle Dave had been there when Sam got home from school. There was nothing odd about that. Since Gran died Uncle Dave often called to see if there was anything his sister wanted him to do. As soon as he got into the house Sam knew there was something wrong. For a start his Mam looked as though she had been crying.

"What's up, Mam?" he'd asked.

Dave put his hand on Sam's shoulder. "You'd better sit down, lad. I want to talk to you."

"Why? I've done nothing, honest."

"I know. Just listen a minute, will you?" Dave took a deep breath. What he had to say wouldn't come easy. "You'll have seen all these folk coming in and out lately; Doctors, Welfare Workers, busy bodies." Sam nodded, wondering what was to come. "They've decided that your Mam's not…" he paused, looking for a kinder explanation than the one that sprang to mind, "well enough," was how he put it, "to look after you."

"We're alright, aren't we, Mam?"

Amy nodded.

"Tell *them* that," Dave's tone was bitter. "Anyway, they've decided that your Mam should go into… " again he paused, " hospital and they wanted to put you in an orphanage but we're not having that, are we Sam?"

Bewildered, Sam shook his head. "You'll come and live with me and your Aunty Hilda. Would you like that?"

Sam didn't answer. He was thinking it over. Cousin Paul was O.K. but that Blanche was a pain in the arse, always wanting her own way - screaming blue murder when she didn't get it. He shrugged.

Dave laughed. "There's enthusiasm for you. Well, I'm afraid you have no option, my lad. It's all arranged. Now, listen. Tomorrow a woman will come to take your Mam to hospital, then you'll have to collect your things and bring them over to our house, so I suggest you go upstairs now and pack what you want to take. Alright? Off you go then."

"I'm going out."

"Oh, no you're not. Upstairs. Right now."

"Mam?"

"Do as your Uncle Dave says, there's a good lad." and the tears welled up again. Sam put his arms around her neck.

"Don't go, Mam. Don't let them take you into hospital. I'll look after you. I will, Mam, I promise."

Her arms held him tightly for a moment. "Oh, Sammy love, I wish I could stay with you but they won't let me."

Sam put his head on her shoulder and wondered who 'they' were. If I got the chance I'd murder 'em, he thought. then 'they' couldn't take Mam away.

Sitting on the ground with his back to the trunk of the tree now, Sam went over what had happened the previous day. Aunty Hilda had come round early and helped his

Mam to wash and dress then she'd picked up all the dirty clothes and put them in a bag. "Where's your things, Sam?" Sam pointed to the cardboard box on his bed. "Is that all?" he nodded. Hilda shook her head despairingly. "Come on, then. They're here."

The big black car parked outside the house had the words, "Redburn District Health Authority' emblazoned on the side. It disgorged its passengers - two women in nurses uniform. Gently they helped his mother down the steps.

Dave hugged his sister, "You'll be alright, Amy, love." then turning he asked, "Where's Sam?"

Sam had slithered his way into the back seat of the car.

"Out you come, young man," one of the nurses took his arm and guided him firmly onto the pavement. "You can come and see your mother when she's settled in, O.K?"

"Mam!" Sam wailed. "Mam, let me come with you."

But his mother, always acquiescent, sadly shook her head. "They won't let you, Sammy love." and she began to cry again.

"You're upsetting your mother, Sam. Now you go with your Uncle here, and we'll see you soon, there's a good boy."

Dave held Sam against him as they watched the car disappear round the corner. "It'll be alright, lad, you'll see."

That night Sam lay between clean white sheets with a clean white pillowcase beneath his head. He lay with his hands clasped behind his neck looking up at a clean white ceiling in a room neat and tidy, smelling of lavender. What he would have given to be back in his old room with the grubby bedding, grey ceiling and his clothes strewn across the floor. It had all come so suddenly. If he'd just had time to think, time to see off these 'they' his Uncle Dave talked about he could still be home with his Mam. Thinking of his Mam and what they had done to her made Sam angry. 'They' weren't going to get away with it. Tomorrow he'd go and fetch his Mam out of that hospital. Tomorrow he'd take her home and look after her himself. He'd wash up and tidy his things away. He'd do the shopping and even learn to cook. If Mam was poorly he'd go for the doctor. Dr Walsh would make his Mam better. He could trust Dr Walsh. With this plan in mind Sam fell asleep.

That was yesterday and this morning Aunty Hilda had put out clean clothes for him ready for school.

"Come straight home for your dinner, Sam." and she'd kissed him lightly on the forehead.

But Sam, although he set off in the direction of the school, made a quick detour round the block and headed for his old home at number twelve. That was when he found the two men emptying the house. How dare they! Mam might be coming home soon, then where would they go?

The day dragged on while Sam sat mulling over his fate. How was he going to bring his Mam home now? There'd be no beds to lie on; no chairs to sit on; nowhere to eat the meals he had been going to cook. The thought of food made Sam feel hungry. He ate the chocolate and then he slept.

Later, much later, Sam awoke to the sound of Paul's voice.

"Where d'you think you've been?" Paul yanked his young cousin roughly to his feet. "We've been looking all over for you, you idiot. D'you know what time it is? It's five o'clock."

Sam stared mutely back. He just wanted to be alone.

"He's there, is he?" Dave called from the path and bounded over the grass to where the two boys stood. He looked down at his nephew wondering what to do with him. Grimly he bent towards the boy. "Now look, Sam, I know it's been rough on you these past few days but you have to consider other folks, you know. We're trying to help you, you daft little bugger. Your Aunty Hilda had your dinner ready for you at twelve o'clock. She's been worried sick and she has enough to do without you making things worse. Now you can come home and you'll say you're sorry to her or else you'll find yourself in that orphanage. Savvy?" Sam hung his head. "Well, do you?"

The boy nodded, "Sorry Uncle Dave. I didn't think anybody would care where I'd gone."

"Well we do. Now come home and have something to eat. You must be starving."

Sam said nothing about the chocolate or the money,

"So, you've found him." Aunty Hilda looked formidable. "If this is the way he's going to behave he can go. I'm not putting up with this sort of behaviour. And I mean that."

Sam had visions of the big dormitory and the bullying older boys like he'd seen in that film on the tele. He shuddered and came to the decision that he'd have to use all his guile to get back in Aunty Hilda's good books. "I'm sorry, Aunty Hilda, I am, honest. I just went home to make sure Mam hadn't come back from the hospital and then.....I....I...went to the park to say my prayers and I must have fallen asleep. Mam said I must say my prayers every night and I forgot last night, so…." big innocent eyes awash with tears looked up at her and his voice rose in the agony of his distress. "I want my Mam."

Paul looked at his father and smirked as he saw his mother melt under this performance. Although, to be honest, Sam's distress was real enough, he certainly made the most of it.

"Oh! you poor little mite." Hilda knelt beside him and held him close. "Don't cry, love. Let's wash your face and then we'll have our tea."

Dave grinned and shook his head.

Life at Uncle Dave's wasn't as bad as Sam had at first imagined. At least here he got regular meals. After his Gran died his mother's attempts at cooking had been disastrous. She'd served up meals that even Sam couldn't eat. Eventually she'd given up altogether so that the only hot meal they had was fish and chips, otherwise Sam had to fend for himself - beans on toast, jam and bread, an occasional fried egg laced with lumps of shell. Sometimes, in desperation, he would pinch an apple or a banana from the greengrocer's shop next to the school, or he'd cadge sweets from the other boys. Now he was never hungry. Now he ate regular hot meals and he would have been the first one to admit, had he been asked, that Aunty Hilda was a very good cook.

As far as the other side of life was concerned, after that first 'set to' with his Aunt, Sam had learned how to get round her. It wasn't difficult to play on her sympathy when he found himself on the wrong side of her. Uncle Dave and

Paul were OK. The only drawback was Blanche. She was as clever as Sam at manipulating her mother and they soon realised that, in this, they were two of a kind. They both liked their own way and would go to great lengths to get it but Sam was wise enough to realise that Blanche, being a girl and their daughter, had the advantage. He knew he must tread carefully where she was concerned. Blanche was also aware of her advantage and rode roughshod over young Sam, taunting and teasing him mercilessly.

"Do you know what Dad did with your rabbits, eh?" Blanche smirked. Sam guessed something unpleasant was coming so he said nothing but when she said. "You know that stew we had yesterday? That was…" Sam felt his stomach lurch and turned pale.

Paul put his hand roughly over his sister's mouth, "That's not true, Sam. Don't believe her. Snowy's got a good home, honest."

Later Paul told Sam. "I'll take you to see Snowy if you want, so long as you don't tell anybody, Dad gave her and the young ones to a friend of his who's got a kid in a wheelchair. We can go round the back way and see her over the gate."

"I can't understand our Blanche" Dave told his wife after Sam had been with them a few weeks. "She's always on at Sam. What's up with the lass?"

Hilda shook her head. She'd never noticed anything amiss. Sam and Blanche didn't fight one another, and neither had complained to her, though if they had she couldn't imagine what she could do about it except give them a good talking to. "They're alright. You're imagining things." she told him.

Had Dave asked Paul however, his son could have told him. Paul knew what motivated his sister - it was jealousy. Paul also recognised Sam's caution in dealing with Blanche, knowing his fear that Hilda might carry out her threat to have him put in an orphanage if he didn't behave himself.

"Keep away from our Blanche," Paul advised his cousin, "she's poison, but Mam thinks the sun shines out of her."

Sam wasn't having an easy time of it at school either. Blanche's bile followed him there too.

"Eh, Sam, your Blanche says your Mam's gone barmy," Mark Lowe jeered. "They've put her in the loony bin, haven't they?"

"She's not barmy," Sam yelled, his face red with indignation, "She's in hospital 'cos she's ill."

The shouting drew a crowd of their schoolmates, gathering like hounds for the kill.

"She's a nutter, your Mam."

"Yea, she's gone nuts, she has."

"Don't wonder she's gone off her trolley with a son like you."

"Everybody knows she's barmy. Amy Watson's always been barmy. My Mam said"

Sam was near to tears but tears aren't allowed for ten-year old boys, not in front of his peers.

"You're lying - all of you. I hate you," and he lunged at his nearest tormentor, who happened to be Mark. The blow caught the boy full in the face, and with a howl Mark retaliated. This was the signal for the start of a free-for-all. Sam found himself at the receiving end of a barrage of blows from half-a-dozen or more of his classmates.

"OK. that's enough." Paul shouted above the din, at the same time dragging two of the boys off his cousin. "Now hop it, the lot of you, and leave him alone." Paul's air of authority and the fact that he was two years older than the others, had the desired effect of breaking up the fight. The boys slunk away muttering dire threats.

"What was that all about, then?"

"They said Mam was in the loony bin and she's not. She's not, is she Paul?" Sam rubbed his bruises. "They're all liars, the lot of em."

"Come on, let's go and have our tea." Paul put his arm around Sam's shoulders and led him home.

"It's time I had a chat with Sam," Dave told Hilda later that evening while he helped with the washing up, "Paul says he's been having trouble with the kids at school."

"What's he been doing now?" Hilda sounded weary.

"He's done nothing." Dave glared at his wife. "Why do you always suppose everything is his fault?"

"I don't, but he seems always to be up to his ears in trouble. So what's this about?"

"His mother."

Hilda looked up sharply at her husband.

He nodded, "Yes, they've got word that she's in a mental home and they're baiting him about it."

"I suppose you'd better explain to him what it's all about, though I doubt your telling him will help."

"It's better he knows the truth, though, don't you think?

Everyone else seems to know," and he went in search of his nephew.

Sam was watching television when Dave called him into the front room, "Yes, Uncle Dave?"

"Come here a minute, lad." and when Sam entered to room, "Sit down, I want a word with you. No, nothing's wrong," he raised a hand when Sam tried to interrupt. "It's this fight you had at school today. About your Mam, wasn't it.?"

"Paul's been telling you."

Dave nodded, "He's worried about you."

"They said she's gone barmy."

"That's not exactly true, Sam."

His nephew gave him a puzzled look. It was the word 'exactly' that caught his attention.

"Look, Sam, your Mam *is* in a mental home." again he held up his hand when Sam tried to protest. "Lots of people have to go into these places from time to time. Some stay only a short while if they get well again. Others, well, sometimes people need to be looked after a long time. Your Mam has never been… what shall I say.." he changed tack, "..well, she's always been easily led, if you understand. We could never let her play out on her own when she was a child. She'd wander off. Go with anybody. She has always been too willing to please everybody, you know that. She would do anything anybody told her to do. Your Gran always looked after you and Amy and when she died your Mam just couldn't cope. She couldn't look after herself properly never mind you. Your Aunty Hilda and me, we tried to keep an eye on things but you must have realised what a mess the house was in. You didn't get any proper meals either, did you? Anyway, somebody reported it to the Medical Officer of Health and from then on…well, you know what happened."

Sam sat with his chin down on his chest so that Dave couldn't see what his reactions were.

"I thought I'd better tell you how things are. I should have told you before perhaps. I just didn't think anybody would be so nasty as to bait you about your Mam."

"I love my Mam." Sam's voice was barely above a whisper.

"I love her too, Sam. She's my little sister." he took Sam in his arms and let him cry softly on his shoulder. After a while Dave drew him away, "Now, if them lads start on you again, you've just got to ignore 'em. You Mam's not mad. We both know that. No, Sam, she's not mad, just not responsible. You know what I mean?"

Sam wasn't sure that he did know what his uncle meant. He only knew that at times like this he was desperately in need of his mother. When she was there he knew he could find sympathy if things went wrong. Even though she said very little Sam knew she loved him and she was there to comfort him. That's what Mam's are for, isn't it? But now she wasn't there any more and though Dave had shown that he understood, it still wasn't the same. It was his Mam he needed.

"How did it go?" Hilda asked when at last they were alone.

"You know me. I'm not one for making speeches, not even to kids."

Hilda laughed. "Don't I though. I remember your efforts at telling Paul about the birds and the bees."

Dave laughed with her. "He knew more about it than I did. Seriously though, I think Sam understands now. He's a bright kid."

Sam was loathe to go to school after the previous day's incident. He considered playing truant again but decided the result of that would only get him in his Aunty Hilda's black books and he would still have to go back sometime. So it was with a cold feeling in his stomach that he passed through the school gates the next day. He made straight for the wall at the side of the school building and stood with his back to it, one foot braced against the brickwork. praying nobody would notice him. His luck was out. Mark Lowe was looking for him. As he approached Sam saw the result of the previous day's fight. Mark had the blackest eye he'd ever seen. Sam edged along the wall.

Mark said, "Hi, Sam!"

Sam didn't answer. He just nodded. The other boy stood awkwardly in front of him, standing first on one leg and then on the other. "Mam says I have to say sorry for what I said yesterday." Sam let the breath slowly out of his lungs. "She said it was a cruel thing to say and that I deserved my black eye."

"I did that?"

"Dad says you'd make a good boxer."

"He did?"

Relief at the relaxed tension made the boys behave like idiots. Sam giggled and put up his fists. Mark took the same stance and they sparred jokingly.

That was when Paul appeared on the scene.

"You two at it again?" he was ready to separate the pair.

"We're only messing about, Paul," Sam winked at Mark, "His Dad says I'd make a good boxer."

"You're not big enough," Paul laughed.

"I'd be a fly weight."

"More like a flea weight."

"Yes, and I'd bite 'em till they were covered in big red lumps."

"…and black eyes." put in Mark.

The black eye made Mark into quite a celebrity.

"Wow! What a shiner."

"How d'you get that?"

"You look like Henry Cooper after his fight with Mohamed Ali."

Even Mr Bateman remarked, "That's quite a colourful eye you've got there, Mark. How's the other chap?"

"Still out for the count, sir," bragged Mark.

Sam stood aside during all this banter, thankful there would be no reprisals.

CHAPTER 2

Amy sat in the big armchair, in the big room, in the company of the other patients and their visitors. Some chatted excitedly with their relatives and friends while others sat gazing into space or nodding and grinning inanely. The room smelled of urine and disinfectant. Sam eyed the scene with distaste and not a little fear. Would his Mam become like one of these? The thought was unbearable and he turned to run but Dave stood in his way, seeming to sense the boy's distress.

"Hang on there, Sam. It's not as bad as it looks. Come on. Your Mam's over there, look."

Amy looked across at them and waved her hand. Sam flung himself into her arms.

"Mam! Oh, Mam!"

Hilda held a handkerchief to her eyes, while Dave looked on embarrassed.

"How are you, Amy?" he asked.

"Alright." she smiled sadly, and though she was now cleaner and tidier than he'd seen her since before their mother died - her hair combed - not that straw-like frizz he'd been used to seeing lately - her finger nails clean and neatly cut, he realised his sister was far from happy. He tried to console himself with the thought that it was early days yet. She just hadn't had time to settle in, neither had the doctors had time to assess her condition. He told himself she'd be alright but in his heart he knew this wasn't so.

Sam sat close to his mother, holding tight to her hand.

"How's my little Sammy? Have you been good boy?"

Hilda spoke before Sam had time to answer. "Yes. Amy. He's fine, He's eating well and he seems to be settling down with us. Don't you worry about Sam, Amy."

"Good. That's good, isn't it, Sammy love?"

For answer Sam said, "When are you coming home, Mam?

"I don't know, love. They haven't said. "

Sam threw out his chest and stood up. "I'll ask 'em, shall I?" ever willing to defend his mother, even though he still couldn't figure out who 'they' were.

"Leave it, Sam," Dave put a restraining hand on his nephew's shoulder, "Just a bit longer, eh? Now don't you think your Mam's looking better already?"

"No." Sam was feeling angry and bewildered.

"Nevertheless, she'll have to stay."

Sam was about to protest when a fat youth strode up and put his face close to Sam's. "Hello! Who are you?"

Sam drew back, glaring into the plump face. "Go away," he hissed.

"O.K." and the youth shambled off, flapping his hands as he went.

"That's Geoffrey," Amy said, "He's a nice boy."

The conversation during the hour they spent there was desultory and strained, although Amy seemed not to notice. She sat smiling down at her son, just happy to see him again; happy to be with him.

When, much to Dave's relief, the bell shrilled, signalling the end of visiting time, he got up.

"Right, then! Come on, Sam. Time to go."

"I'm staying with Mam."

"Come on, now. Don't start." Dave gently but firmly hoisted his nephew from the chair, and when Sam resisted, "Don't push it, son." for all the softness of his voice there was a warning note there too.

"We'll come again soon, love," Hilda bent to kiss Amy's cheek. "Say goodbye to your Mam, now. There's a good boy."

Sam's arms locked around his mother's neck, unwilling to leave her.

"Right," Dave's hands lifted Sam upright. "I'm warning you, young man, if you make a fuss they won't let you come to see your Mam again."

Slowly, sadly, Sam turned from his mother but at the door he broke away from Dave's grasp and rushed back to Amy.

"I'll come again tomorrow, Mam."

Amy nodded and smiled, the tears wet on her cheeks.

"What's up with him?" Sam looked up from the meal he was toying with. Blanche rarely used his name but he knew she was referring to him by the tone of her voice. "Been to see his Mam, has he?"

"Now, Blanche," her father warned, "Leave Sam alone. He's a bit upset."

She mocked, *"Leave him alone, he's a bit upset."* her voice took on a peevish note. "You're always sticking up for him. I don't matter any more. It's all Sam this and Sam that, but everybody knows what he is," she hesitated before she said, "He's a bastard."

There was a shocked silence for a second or two then Dave leaned across the table and slapped his daughter hard across the face. "Don't you ever say anything like that again, my girl."

Blanche stared at her father in stunned silence then she let out a piercing scream and, holding her cheek, she fled from the room.

"No." Hilda glared at her husband, "and don't you ever hit her again."

"So, you'd let her get away with a nasty remark like that, would you? No," he went on, "it wasn't nasty, it was a downright wicked thing to say."

"There are other ways of…"

"She's always picking on Sam," Paul joined the fray. "She's jealous, that's what's up with her. Sam's never done anything to deserve that."

"Hasn't he?" Hilda's face was red with rage. "Well, I'll tell you this, young man, ever since he's been in this house there's been nothing but trouble. We were a happy family before he came."

"That's not fair, Mam. Any trouble there's been has never been Sam's fault and you know it."

Through all this Sam sat ashen faced and silent, then without a word or a look at anyone he ran from the room and out of the back door. Paul got up to follow him.

"Leave him be," Dave said, "Let him alone for a bit." and when Paul hesitated, "Finish your meal, son. He'll be back."

But Paul couldn't eat. The unfairness of this attack on Sam was more than he could stomach.

"I'm going after him," he said. But when Paul got

outside the gate there was no sign of his cousin.

Sam's heart beat fast as he ran down the road. He had no idea where he was going, he just had to get away from that house where they hated him. He knew if he went back it would mean the orphanage and he would never go there. Never. He ran until he was exhausted. Sitting on a garden wall he waited until he got his breath back and he could think more clearly what to do and where to go. It would be dark in an hour or two and he had to find somewhere to sleep. The park and the willow tree were out of the question. It was too cold to sleep there for one thing and he hated to be alone in the park when it was dark anyway. Then the idea came. But of course! He'd go back home. There he'd have time to think and plan and they'd never imagine he would go back to an empty house. More slowly this time he set out for number twelve.

It came as a bit of a shock to find two workmen there. A lorry stood outside and the men were busy boarding up the windows. What they want to do that for? Sam asked himself. Now how was he to get in? As he watched, one of the men got down from his ladder and went to the back of the house to reappear a moment later carrying a plank of wood. Sam heard him shout to his mate.

"We'll need some more timber, Frank."

"Right, Joe. I'll go and get a load from the yard."

"...and don't muck about down there. It's nearly time to knock off."

The second man, who answered to the name of Frank, jumped into the lorry and drove off, leaving the gate wide open. Sam edged nearer. Joe climbed the ladder with the plank under one arm, giving

Sam the opportunity to slip unseen through the gate and round the back of the house. He turned the handle on the back door. It was locked.

"Dammit!" he muttered and looked around to see if anyone was watching. Only Mr Makin next door raked his vegetable patch. Old Makin was OK. It was his missus who was the nosey one. Sam crouched down and lifted the big flower pot at the edge of the path. Yes, the key was still there. It took no time at all to unlock the door and slip inside. Up the stairs he went, careful not to go near the front bedroom were the man was busy nailing the batten to the outside of the window frame. In what had been Sam's bedroom, empty now, swept clear of all the rubbish that had been left, he sat down on the floor. He must think. Where could he go? Wherever it was he had to let his Mam know. Would she tell? No. Not if he asked her not to - just so long as she knew he was alright. He felt in his trouser pocket and took comfort from the fact that he hadn't spent all of the ten shillings the workman had given him. Besides that he had another two shillings his Uncle Dave had given him yesterday.

Sam settled down to wait.

When he heard the scrape of a ladder against the wall outside his window panic gripped him. They'd see him when they reached the windowsill. The cupboard on the landing - that was his only chance. With the agility of youth Sam was out of the bedroom and into the cupboard, pulling the door to behind him before the man reached the windowsill. He was careful not to let the catch close. That would mean he wouldn't be able to get out. He'd been caught like that once before. For what seemed like hours he sat hunched on the bottom shelf, listening. Eventually he heard the ladder being taken down, the lorry start up and drive away. Only then did he dare to come out of hiding. Stiffly he jumped down from the shelf and peered through the slit in the wood. Satisfied that they had really gone he stretched his cramped body on the floor, reasoning that if he could sleep now, he'd be less tired when it came time for him to make his move.

A voice calling 'Bobby! Bobby!', woke him. Sam rubbed his eyes. It must be nine o'clock. Mrs Makin always called her cat for his supper at nine o'clock. The daylight had gone. No light showed through the chink in the shutters. He was thirsty - very thirsty. The bathroom was his first stop but when he tried to flush the toilet nothing happened. After a vain effort to get a drink in the kitchen he realised the water had been turned off and he poked around under the sink for the stop tap. He tried to turn it but it was too stiff for his small fingers so he picked up a piece of wood the men had discarded, banging it against the stop tap. He managed to turn it slightly, just enough to allow a trickle of water to dribble from the tap. Cupping his hands he let the cool water fill his palms and gulped it down, soothing his dry throat. What a pity he hadn't eaten before he left Uncle Dave's. He thought about the food he'd left on the plate and groaned. He was starving. Still, he had that money in his pocket. The off-licence would still be open. He'd get something there. Feeling his way to the back door he turned the key only to find that, like the windows, it had been boarded up. He pushed hard at the boards but to no avail. Time and again he flung himself against the battens until he was exhausted. He gave up. That was it, he thought, he was trapped forever. When they came to open the house in about a hundred years from now, they would find just his bones lying there all bloody. Then they'd all be sorry for what they'd said, especially Blanche. It was a wonder to Sam how anyone as pretty as she was could be so horrible. Paul was the only one he cared about - Paul and his Mam. His Mam would be sorry, he knew. Sam slithered his back down the wall and sat on the floor. Maybe his Mam would tell them off for being so mean with him but he knew deep down inside him that she wouldn't say anything. She would just cry.

...

"Have you found him?" Hilda asked anxiously.

Dave shook his head.

"He's not in his usual hiding place," Paul sank down on the nearest chair.

"…and we've looked everywhere else we can think of." Dave added, "It's nearly dark. I think we ought to call the police."

"No, Dave, not yet. I don't want the police coming here. What will the neighbours say?"

"You astonish me, woman. A young lad's lost, maybe in danger, even dead, and you worry about the neighbours. But then maybe you're frightened they'll find out why he ran away. If the truth comes out that you and that daughter of yours brought this on…"

"I did no such thing."

"Yes, Mam, you said he'd caused a lot of trouble since he came to live with us."

"Well," Hilda looked down at the hands that twitched nervously on her lap, "I didn't mean for him to run off like that. Maybe I shouldn't have said it but after you hit our Blanche… and any way, it's what I think."

"It wasn't his fault they were thrown out of their house," Paul's voice was hoarse with anger, "It wasn't his fault the kids picked on him at school. It was our Blanche that told everybody about Aunty Amy, and you can't blame Sam for being upset. He'd be a hard case if he wasn't."

"I know, love. I know. I'm sorry. That's just it. I feel sorry for him and mad at him in turns." Hilda shook her head, "The whole business of Amy being put away has been a nightmare."

Paul put his arms around his mother and said gently, "We've got to find him, Mam."

"Yes, of course we have. You'd better tell the police, Dave."

"I'll go down to the station, then they won't have to send anybody here 'til later - 'til they've found him."

Blanche crept downstairs. There was fear in her eyes. "Have they found him, Mam?"

Hilda shook her head.

"He's probably thrown himself in the river after the way you've treated him."

"That's enough, our Paul. Nobody's suggesting he's done any such thing."

"Mam, I'm sorry," Blanche's voice trembled on the brink of tears. "I'm really sorry - honest."

Paul eyed his sister with disbelief. Sorry for herself, he thought.

…

It had been a long night for Sam. He was afraid of being alone in the house. The floorboards creaked, windows rattled, the wind moaned down the chimney and the tap's drip, drip had sounded ever louder as the night went on. To add to his misery hunger gnawed at his belly, convincing him that he would starve to death. He must have slept for, as the sun rose and a streak of light crept across the floor, Sam opened his eyes and for a moment wondered where he was. He struggled stiffly to his feet and peered out into the street. Everything was still. Only the birds sang. Once more he attacked the battens on the door. They wouldn't budge. Disconsolately he shuffled into the kitchen and drank from the dripping tap. It was while he bent over the sink that he heard the rattle of milk bottles. That would be Ron. Should he call for help? If he attracted too much attention Sam knew he'd be dragged back to his Uncle Dave's, or worse, the police would come. Anyway, Mam owed Ron for the milk so he was hardly likely to help. By now Sam was desperately hungry. He must do something before death claimed him. That was Gran's phrase. She always talked about death claiming folk. 'Yes,' she'd say, 'death claimed your Grandad before he was fifty. That's no age for a man to die.' Ten's no age, either, Sam thought. He had to do something now, before it was too late.

It had occurred to Sam last night that he might knock on the wall to the Makins'. After all the old bat was always doing it for him to be quiet, only he knew Mrs Makin would blab to everybody. She never could keep her mouth shut about anything. The old man, on the other hand might just take pity on him and let him out. Then, once outside he would make a dash for it before they had chance to tell anybody where he was. Yes, that was it - brilliant! He knocked now with his fist but it had little effect, besides it hurt his knuckles. Then he remembered the piece of wood he'd used to turn the stop tap. Bang! Bang! Bang! If that didn't wake them, Sam thought, nothing would.

"Walter!" Mrs Makin shook her husband awake, "Walter, did you hear that?" Mr Makin was a mite deaf. "Listen," she said impatiently. Bang! Bang! Bang! "It's coming from next door."

"There's nobody there. It's empty. Boarded up."

"You heard it. Surely you heard that."

Mr Makin turned over and tried to get back to sleep.

Bang! Bang! Bang!

"There it is again, Walter. D'you think it's Amy haunting the place?"

"Amy's not dead, you stupid woman. It'll be the wind. They've left a board loose."

Bang! Bang! Bang! Then a scream "OW! OOH! OW!"

Walter turned over and looked at his wife. "That's not the wind."

Sam had trapped his fingers between the wall and the piece of wood. "OOH! OW! ME 'AND." He squealed.

"If I didn't know any better I'd say that was young Sam's voice."

"It can't be. How on earth…?"

Bang! Bang! Bang!

Walter picked up his slipper. Bang! Bang! Bang! he retaliated. "I'll tan your backside, you young bugger."

"Help! Mr Makin, I'm locked in," but Walter couldn't

hear.

"D'you know what time it is?"

Bang! Bang! Bang! Sam wasn't going to give up now.

"I'll skelp you, I will." Walter vowed.

"How's he got in there, anyway?" Annie Makin asked.

"I don't know, do I? And I don't care. I just want to go back to sleep."

Bang! Bang! Bang!

"Right! That does it." and Walter slipped his trousers over his pyjamas, went out into the garden and round to number twelve.

Sam heard the Makins' back door slam and Walter struggle over the fence; at least he heard the language Walter always used when he strode across the piece of wood that served to divide the gardens of number twelve and number fourteen and he heard the crunch of his shoes on the path below the kitchen window. Sam was at the back door before Mr Makin reached it, banging with the bit of wood on the shutters.

"I'm fastened in, Mr Makin," he shouted, "LET ME OUT."

"I thought it was you, you young devil. How did you get yourself nailed up in there?"

"Let me out, PLEASE."

"Can't hear you, lad. Speak up. Are you alright?"

Sam yelled louder. "YES. JUST GET ME OUT."

"Get you out." Walter Makin was enjoying this. He smiled to himself. Here was retribution. Now the time had come to repay all those tricks Sam had played on him. Like the time he'd pinched all the strawberries from his garden while he and his wife were out, and the time he'd let his rabbit through the fence and it had eaten most of the lettuces…and the time… Oh yes! Now was the time to get his own back. "Can't do that, lad. You'll have to wait 'til the Council Offices open at 9 o'clock…unless," he said as an afterthought, "..unless I fetch t'bobby."

Sam was silent. He didn't want to get in trouble with the police. That would be the end. They'd lock him up and then he'd never get away. It would be prison or the orphanage for him.

"No, don't tell the police. PLEASE. I'll wait. I won't bang on the wall any more. But you won't forget, will you?"

"I won't forget." Walter Makin tittered to himself all the way back home.

"Them silly buggers from the Council have boarded the place up with the lad inside. It wouldn't occur to them to have a look round before they nailed the door up, would it?"

"I can't believe it. He must have got in there after they'd gone."

"You do talk some rubbish. If he got in after they'd gone, then why can't he get out the same way, tell me that , woman?"

Mrs Makin looked perplexed. "I don't know, do I? You've been round there. I haven't. You should know."

Mr Makin shook his head sadly and gave up the struggle. "Anyway, I've told him he'll have to wait 'til t'Council folk can come to let him out."

"We can't leave him there 'til 9 o'clock gone. Dave'll be frantic over him by now. You'll have to get your clothes on and go round there. Tell 'em what's happened."

Her husband looked at her in disgust. "It's half-past-six" he squeaked, "It's the middle of the night as far as I'm concerned."

"You've got to go."

"Bloody kid. He's alus up to summat," Walter Makin's sour look spoke volumes. "Make us a cup o' tea while I get me clothes on."

Dave was getting ready for work after a long sleepless night of worrying about his nephew when Sergeant Gill knocked on the door.

"We've done a search of the area," he said as he stepped into the hall, "but there's no sign of him yet."

Dave's face was drawn and anxious, "Come in Sergeant. We've just made another pot of tea."

"Thanks, Mr Watson. It's none too warm out there yet." the sergeant sat on the edge of the easy chair balancing the cup and saucer on his knee. He could see the strain and exhaustion clearly written on Hilda's face. "Look, Mrs Watson, these kids run off in the heat of the moment but they come home when their belly's empty.Try not to worry, it's not often they come to any harm." Sergeant Gill said reassuringly..

Dave shook his head , "We've looked everywhere we can think of. We've even been back to his old home but it's all boarded up. He couldn't have got in there - not a chance. We've been to his usual hideout in the park too, though it would have been a bit cold sleeping out there last night. We don't know where else to look."

Hilda stood by the window where she'd spent most of the night. She spoke now for the first time.

"Old Mr Makin's coming. Maybe he's got news for

us." Before Walter could lift the knocker Hilda was at the door. "Have you seen him? Have you seen Sam, Mr Makin?"

"Aye, I have."

"Come in. Come in. We've had the police out looking for him all night. The sergeant's here now."

"Police? No, I'll not talk to the police. I promised t'lad, you see."

"Why? Where is he? What's he done?"

Mr Makin lowered his voice. "He's got himself boarded up in number twelve. Them silly sods from t'Council boarded t'windows and t'doors up wi' 'im inside. He's been there all night - couldn't get out."

Despite this whispered account the sergeant heard what the old man said. He stood behind Hilda and a nerve twitched in his cheek. "Boarded up in an empty house, is he?"

"You might as well come in and tell Sergeant Gill about it now."

Walter stepped over the threshold and another cup of tea was handed out.

Hilda was crying and laughing. "Oh! I am glad. I do thank you Mr Makin."

"Naye, lass. I could do no less than let you know as soon as we heard him," and he related the story of the morning's events.

"So where is he now?" the sergeant asked. "Frightened to come home, is he?"

"Naye. He's still boarded up."

The sergeant spluttered into his cup. After a coughing fit he said, "We'll have to get him out then, won't we?"

"Well, you see, Sergeant, he's scared to death you'll arrest him. But it weren't lad's fault, really. He just went there to hide while he got over what was bothering him."

"Don't worry. There'll be no charges," he was already turning over in his mind how he would relate this story to his mates back at the station. It would make a bit of light relief after some of the grim tales that were told there.

"How do you manage it, Sam?" Dave asked when they brought him home. "How do you manage to get into so much trouble?"

"Dunno," Sam said with his mouth full of toast.

CHAPTER 3

Sam tried so hard to fit in with this family in the weeks that followed but some of the things they expected of him, apart from putting up with Blanche, were to his way of thinking totally unnecessary. To wash his hands three or four times a day, for instance, and to have a bath every night seemed a complete waste of time to Sam. His mother had never made him wash if he didn't want to but here everybody did it, even Uncle Dave. Another thing that irked Sam was the fact that he had to come straight home from school for his meals - no messing about with his mates and wandering in when he felt like it. Now he had to keep himself tidy - socks pulled up, shirt buttons fastened, school tie straight, not pulled off and stuffed in his pocket. Now he had to be in at a reasonable time in the evening - no roaming the streets till all hours. All these things he had to put up with if he wanted to stay. The only compensation to Sam's way of thinking, was his Aunty Hilda's cooking. The meat and potato pies, the steak and kidney puddings that she served up were smashing, and the chocolate pudding, the rice pudding and the jam rolypoly were even better than those his Gran used to make.

So Sam settled into life with the Watsons. His fear of being sent to the orphanage was allayed when Hilda told him, "I'm sorry if you thought I would send you away, Sam. I didn't mean it. It's not been easy for any of us, least of all you, I know. Now why don't we make a fresh start, you and me?" she put her arm around his shoulder. "Kiss and make up, eh?"

Dutifully Sam kissed her cheek. What a soppy thing to have to do, he thought. Dave smiled benignly at them both. "Yes, Sam, we'll all start afresh but just remember what Sergeant Gill told you. Running away doesn't solve any problems. You have to face up to them. So if anything's worrying you, lad, just come and talk it over with me. Alright?"

Sam nodded. He knew, all the same, that some of the things bothering him couldn't be resolved by talking them over with his uncle; Blanche, for instance. Although the atmosphere was less fraught, there was no love lost between the two of them. There was a gulf that neither could or would bridge.

Paul on the other hand was a real friend to Sam. Paul understood how he felt, understood the hurt when they took his mother away and again when he found out where they had taken her. He certainly understood the problems Sam still faced with Blanche.

"She's a spoilt brat," he told Sam. "It's because she's a girl. She's always got away with murder. What she needs is a few more slaps like the one Dad gave her. Gosh! That really shook her. He's never hit her before." Paul laughed. "Didn't tell you she was real worried when you didn't come home, did I?"

"Worried? About me?"

Paul nodded, "She thought she'd be in more trouble. She hasn't said she's sorry to you though, has she?" Sam shook his head. "But I don't think she knew what it meant, Sam," Paul jibbed at using the word 'bastard' but Sam didn't.

"I know what bastard means, I've been called it often enough, and so does she."

"No, kid, she just knew it was swearing. Like calling someone a pig, or…."

Sam's look told Paul there was no point in defending Blanche, that what he had just said was merely excusing his sister..

And so Sam struggled on, dutifully observing the rules, keeping out of Blanche's way whenever possible, ever thankful for Paul's support. The only bright spot in the week was his visit to see his mother.

Sunday again! Dave hated Sundays. Sunday was the day Dave and Hilda took Sam to see his mother. It wasn't that Dave didn't want to see his sister, it was the hospital; such a dismal place, and he knew Hilda hated it too, which made Dave feel guilty asking her to go. Only Sam looked forward to the hour they spent with Amy. He sat close to her, holding her hand, not saying much, just happy to be with her. When the time came for them to leave Sam would cling to his mother, only loosening his hold when he was pulled away by Dave. Today was no different.

"Come on, Sam. We have to go now."

"When's Mam coming out?" the pain he felt at leaving her all too obvious.

Dave gave a weary sigh, "I don't know, Sam." He hadn't the heart to say "never" which was what the doctor had intimated.

'Miss Watson is autistic' I'm afraid she'll never be any better. There again,' the doctor smiled broadly as though he'd just discovered some important medical breakthrough, 'she probably won't get any worse either.'

Dave knew nothing about autism but he could see with every visit that Amy grew paler and thinner and less inclined to talk. Even when they visited her on Sam's birthday she had to be reminded of the occasion.

"It's my birthday today, Mam," Sam told her, disappointed that she hadn't remembered.

"Your birthday, love? Oh, yes, you're …let me see… you're ten, aren't you?"

"I'm eleven, Mam."

"Eleven?" Amy's smile was sad. "You're growing up without me, Sammy." the tears started in her eyes. "You'll grow up and forget about me."

"No, Mam, I'll never do that. I'll always come and see you. Nobody'll stop me." and he threw his arms around her neck. "Anyway, you'll soon be better and then you can come home and I'll look after you." Fleetingly Sam wondered where they would live, but that was something he'd worry about when the time came. Maybe 'they' would let them have number twelve back. "You'll be home for my next birthday, Mam." he told her.

Sadly Amy patted his hand. "I haven't got you a present or a card, love."

"It doesn't matter, Mam."

"Yes it does. Here, pass me my purse, there's a good boy." and she took out a £5 note, "Get something nice with this, Sammy love."

"Gosh! Thanks, Mam." Sam was overawed at the sight of so much money.

"WHAT ARE YOU DOING?" the Ward Nurse

appeared at Amy's side. "You are not allowed to take money from the patients." Amy cringed visibly. "Give it back immediately."

"Just a minute," Dave intervened, "His mother has every right to give him a birthday present."

"A present, yes. Money's a different matter. It's the rule here."

"Don't be stupid, woman." Hilda joined the argument. "Sam didn't ask for the money. He hasn't stolen it. Now mind your own business."

By now their voices were raised in anger. Amy, her eyes wide, her face pale, started to sob. "He's my baby. He's my baby."

"There now," the nurse patted Amy's shoulder while glaring at Sam." "Look what you've done. I shall have to give her her medication," and she took a bottle of pills from the pocket of her uniform, poured water from the nearby jug and offered it to Amy.

"What's that you're giving her?" Dave asked.

"They're drugging her. I thought she looked as though she was doped when we came last time." Hilda glared menacingly at the woman.

"We have to sedate patients when they get upset. It's the only way we can stop them getting violent."

"VIOLENT!" Dave's voice rose in horror, "My sister's never been violent in her life." he pointed to a weeping Amy. "You can't call that violent. She's always been docile. Too soft for her own good, hasn't she, Hilda?"

"Always."

"Look," the nurse was getting agitated. "Miss Watson must take her medication," and she held out her hand with the pill on her palm. But before Amy could take it from her Sam grabbed it and put it in his mouth.

"No!" the nurse screamed. "Don't swallow it. It could kill you." Sam swallowed hard.

Before anyone could object the woman marched him off to the Sluice Room, put her fingers down his throat and made him vomit. Sam fought her all the way but she was a big woman and used to dealing with difficult patients. By the time Hilda and Dave reached the Sluice Room it was all over.

"There, now," the nurse was saying to a popeyed, gasping Sam. "You'd better have a drink of water."

"How dare you manhandle my nephew like that. You're not going to get away with this, I can tell you. I'm going to see the Matron, and if she won't do anything about your behaviour, I'll take it further." Dave was beside himself with rage. It was all he could do to stop from hitting the woman.

"I've just saved his life, you stupid man, and if I know anything about Matron there'll be no more visits from this young man."

Grabbing Sam's arm, Dave yelled, "We'll see about that. Come on Sam, say goodbye to your mother, we have things to do."

Outside the Ward, still holding his nephew by the arm, Dave said, "Alright, Sam. Hand it over."

"What d'you mean?"

"The pill. Give it to me."

"But…."

"Don't tell me you swallowed it because I know you didn't. I saw you slip it into your pocket and I want it to show the Matron. Then I'll deal with you, young man."

"No you won't," Hilda shook her head at her husband. "He did the right thing. They've no right to dope Amy like that. No wonder she's going down hill all the time."

...

The Matron sat behind a huge old-fashioned desk, her large bosom resting on folded arms.

"Come." she shouted, in answer to Dave's knock but Dave was already inside the door followed by Hilda and Sam. The Nurse was standing to one side of the desk, smirking.

"Well, now, Mr Watson. I believe we've been having trouble with your nephew here."

"On the contrary, Miss…Miss…"

"Jones."

"…Miss Jones, we've been having trouble with this nurse," Dave said, nodding his head in the direction of the other woman.

The Matron smiled sardonically, "You'd better tell me your side of the story, I think. Sit down, please."

Hilda sat on the chair nearest the door with Sam beside her.

"I'd rather stand," Dave felt that to stand over this woman gave him a certain advantage.

"As you wish. Now tell me what happened in your view." she started to toy with the pen on her desk as though to suggest that she was already bored by the subject.

It annoyed Dave. He nodded towards the pen "Do you mind." She desisted. "I think," he took a deep breath ready for the battle of words he knew was to come, "rather than me telling you what happened I'd like to hear what she," he nodded again towards the other woman, "has to say."

Miss Jones hesitated briefly, "Nurse Raymond tells me that she caught this young man taking money from Miss Watson's purse."

Hilda gasped, "That's not true."

"I never."

Dave put up a staying hand, "Let her finish."

"When Nurse Raymond protested, this young man, to put it in the nurse's words 'kicked up a fuss' which upset the patient. The nurse then felt it necessary to give Miss Watson her medication in order to calm her,"

"Drugs you mean," this from Hilda.

The Matron ignored this interruption, "The boy then snatched the pill from the nurse and swallowed it. Nurse Raymond then deemed it necessary, for the boy's sake, to evacuate the pill from his stomach. For that purpose she rushed the boy to the sluice room and did just that. You should be grateful to the nurse. That pill could have had dire consequences for one so young."

"Is that it, then?"

Matron gave a slight nod.

"Then I'll tell you what really happened. Today is Sam's birthday. There was no card or present from his mother - she had forgotten, which naturally made her unhappy, so she offered him a £5 note from her purse. 'Get something nice with this, Sammy, love' were her very words."

The Matron half turned in her chair to face Nurse Raymond, "How come Miss Watson had so much money in her purse?" she asked.

The nurse shook her head. Matron accepted this as a

denial that Nurse Raymond knew anything about the money.

"We don't encourage patients to keep any money apart from a little loose change," she told Dave.

"What would you have done then, if you had known about the money?"

"What we usually do in circumstances like that is to put the money in an envelope with the patient's name on it in the safe."

"You must have thousands in there, then." it was a facetious remark and Dave wished he hadn't put it quite like that.

The woman flushed, "We give it back to the relatives."

"That would be Sam, wouldn't it?"

Matron let out a sigh, "We would have given it to you."

"But you see, Matron, I gave it to Amy in the first place so she could buy a present for her son."

"Really, Mr Watson, we seem to be going round in circles and it still doesn't excuse the boy swallowing the tablet."

"He didn't.

"But…but.."

"I saw him swallow it, Matron." Nurse Raymond spoke for the first time.

Dave took the pill from his pocket and held it on his palm just as the nurse had done when she offered it to Amy, "Could this be the pill you're talking about?"

Matron stared at the pill for a second or two then glared across at Nurse Raymond. "This changes the situation entirely." and she made to take the offending pill from Dave."

"Oh, no! I need this for evidence. I'm going to the Medical Officer of Health with this to show him how you are drugging your patients unnecessarily. These," Dave held the pill between his finger and thumb, "are to calm violent patients, I understand."

"Yes."

"There is no way my sister needs drugs like this. She has never been violent. I've never heard my sister even raise her voice let alone be violent. Depressed she may be but no wonder when you're doping her like this. She isn't mad; she's autistic, according to the doctor here."

"Look, Mr Watson, I don't dispute your story and I shall certainly take issue with Nurse Raymond about this matter. In fact," once more she glared at the nurse. "I rather think Nurse Raymond is unfit for her post."

The woman's face paled, "That's not fair," she burst into tears and fled from the room.

"Whether you sack this woman or not, the fact remains that there hasn't been enough supervision as far as your patients' medication is concerned, has there? And that, I think, is your department." Dave's tone was icy.

The Matron's face flushed once more. She looked down at the blotter on her desk. "I can only apologise."

"That's something anyway," came from Hilda, then, looking at Dave, she said, "We have to get back for Blanche, love."

As they reached the door Dave turned, "I don't expect my sister to be given any more of those drugs and I'll tell you this, Miss Jones, I'm taking this matter further." and he slammed the door behind him.

"Wow! You were great, Uncle Dave."

"You'll see how great I can be when I get you home, my lad."

"Dave, you leave him alone. He did the right thing. It's right he should stand up for his Mam."

With a look of exasperation Dave said, "It's like you said, Hilda, trouble follows this lad around."

CHAPTER 4

Hilda sat at the kitchen table, her chin on her hands looking decidedly worried.

"It's not that I'm being greedy, Dave, but now that your overtime's been cut it's not easy managing on less, especially with an extra mouth to feed. I'm not complaining," Hilda got up from her chair and came round the table to put her hand on Dave's shoulder, "don't think that, love. It's just that, on top of everything else Sam needs a whole lot of new clothes. Those things he brought with him were already second-hand and past redemption. I've done my best to mend them but now they're getting too small and Paul's things are miles too big for him."

It was Dave's turn to look worried, "I don't know what I can do about it, Hilda, I honestly don't."

"Surely Sam's father must still be making him an allowance and after all it is for Sam, not Amy. I was thinking," she paused to nibble at her thumb nail, "perhaps if you went to the Council or the Court, or wherever, and explained things, maybe…"

"There's her bank… but I doubt there'll be any money in that. She'd have paid the rent with it otherwise."

"We'll have to do something, Dave."

Dave frowned and nodded his agreement. "I can try, I suppose. I'll go this morning before I start my shift." It was a task Dave didn't relish.

…

"Well? How did you get on?" Hilda asked after his promised visit to the Magistrates Court.

Dave flopped down on the settee, "Officious lot, they are. They make you feel like you're begging. This chap I saw denied there'd ever been a Court Order. He told me there was nothing on record, and suggested we should apply for Family Allowance for him."

"I never thought about that," Hilda pursed her lips, "I think, though, we'd have to adopt him legally."

"Amy would never agree to that."

"No I don't suppose she would. So what else did this chap say?"

"There's a lot of red tape to go through if we apply for assistance. It'll take ages. They seem to put a whole lot of obstacles in the way." Dave gave a despairing sigh. Then on a lighter note he went on, "I'll tell you what, though. I took myself round to the Town Hall and asked to see a Councillor."

"What good would that do? They weren't any help to Amy, and we never see any of 'em from one election to another."

"You're right but do you know who our Councillor is?" Hilda shook her head. "Roger Wilmott!" Dave waiting for a reaction.

It came with a gasp, "Roger Wilmott?" Dave nodded sagely. "That must have been a bit embarrassing."

"Not for me. He didn't seem to realise who I was - not at first anyway. I kept it impersonal. Told him we were fostering a child who badly needed some new clothes. I explained the mother was in a mental institution and that we couldn't afford to kit him out ourselves. It was when I told him my name that he looked....startled - well, that's putting it mild - more shocked, I'd say,"

"I'm amazed. I really am. D'you think he'll do anything?"

"He'd better."

"I don't understand why you didn't go to him in the first place, after all..."

"I promised Mam, didn't I? She made me swear never to go near him."

"Well that's daft. She might have known Amy would need help when anything happened to her."

"He knows now, anyway. He didn't exactly promise anything. Just said he'd see into it."

...

"That sounds like the post." Hilda looked up from her breakfast the following morning, then looking at her watch, "He's late. Go and see what it is, somebody."

"I'll go," Paul scrambled from the table and hurried into the hall. He came back more slowly holding a bulging foolscap envelope. "It's addressed to Sam." he said in surprise.

"Me?" Sam took the envelope and tore it open spilling the contents over the table.

There was a gasp of surprise. "Wow!" Paul picked up the note nearest to him, "Five quid! How many are there?"

One by one Sam counted the money, "Ten, fifteen, twenty, twenty five, thirty, thirty five, forty, forty five, FIFTY QUID! Gosh! Where did it come from?"

Hilda gave Dave a knowing look. They realised where the money had come from. She asked, "Is there a letter?"

Sam looked inside what was left of the envelope. "No.

Nothing." then he handed one of the notes to Paul and the rest he gave to Dave, "I owe you this, Uncle Dave." tears stung Hilda's eyes. "but you can give us a fiver if you like."

For a full sixty seconds Dave looked down at the bundle of notes in his hand, then he swallowed hard before he said, "Here, lad," and handed back one of the notes to Sam, "but the rest I'm giving to your Aunty Hilda to buy you some new clothes."

Paul handed his money over to his mother too, "I don't need that, kid. You can buy me an ice cream out of your fiver. OK?"

Blanche's sullen expression was proof that she felt left out, "It's probably stolen anyway." she muttered.

"Blanche!" Hilda glared at her daughter, "What a dreadful thing to say."

"We e ell. Why should anybody send him all that money," and she slid off her chair and stalked out of the room.

Dave shook his head, "She's a little bugger, is that one. Never you mind her, Sam. I'm very pleased for you."

"I was going to get her something out of this fiver," Sam screwed up the note and stuffed it into his pocket, "only she…" he didn't finish what he was going to say, realising his remark wouldn't have gone down very well with his Aunt."

"You'll lose it cramming it into your pocket like that," Hilda said quickly, following Sam's train of thought . "Put it in your room until you want to spend it."

Saturday morning found Hilda and Sam in the town

centre.

"Come on, Sam, in here." and Hilda pushed him gently through the revolving doors of the big store and up the escalator into the men's department.

"Can I help you, madam?" the assistant asked.

"I want to fit this young man out with some new clothes. I think we'll start with a suit."

The young man looked disdainfully down at Sam's attire. "Yes, madam. This way."

They followed the assistant until he stopped beside a row of boys' suits on a long rail. Hilda looked through the suits lifting out one after another until she came across one she thought would be the right size.

Sam stood by looking bored.

"We'll try this one," she said holding the suit up to Sam's shoulder, "Yes, we'll try this."

Sam almost panicked, "What was she on about, '*We'll* try this one.' She wasn't going to try it on, was she?"

"The fitting room's this way, madam,"

"Must I?" Sam whined.

"Yes, you must. It's no use buying clothes if they won't fit, is it?"

The shop assistant held back the curtain and stood aside for Sam and Hilda to pass. Sam's look of alarm made Hilda smile. "I can manage, Aunty Hilda." Sam quickly nipped inside the cubicle and drew the curtain across the rail.

A few minutes later he came out wearing the suit, his hair ruffled. Automatically Hilda smoothed it down, and that small gesture went to Sam's heart. Suddenly he hugged her. She laughed, "What was that about?" but she already knew. She realised that there hadn't been enough physical contact between her and the boy. Poor Sam, she thought, he must have been missing his mother's love terribly. She hugged him back, kissing his forehead. "Now, let's look at you." Holding him at arms length she inspected his new suit. "It fits alright, Sam. Do you like it?"

Sam nodded. He'd never owned a suit before. It made him feel quite grown up.

"We have to get shirts and socks, another pair of trousers and you need some new underwear too."

"I'll be glad when we've done with this lot." Sam grinned at her.

The contact between them had lessened the tension and given Sam the confidence to speak up.

"It won't take long but neither will it be the last time, young man . Clothes don't last forever, you know."

"Till I've left school, anyway."

"You're joking. Not the way you're growing. Where did your Mam take you for your clothes?"

"She didn't. They were what folks gave me."

Hilda looked at her nephew. Poor lamb, what a life he's had, she thought, and made up her mind that things would be different for him from now on.

CHAPTER 5

"Hilda, have you moved my watch?"

"No, love. It's on the sideboard where you left it."

"It isn't."

"It must be. I saw it there only a few minutes since."

"Well, it's not there now." Dave bellowed so that the whole household could hear him, "Who's moved my watch?"

A chorus of, "Not me." "Not me." "Not me." came from upstairs.

"I'm going to be late for work and I need that watch."

"Take mine."

"Wear a woman's watch. Not on your life."

Paul came downstairs jumping the last four steps. "Here, Dad. You can take mine. Can I wear yours if I find it?"

"No, you can't. That watch was a present from your Mam and I don't want it smashed up or lost."

"You *have* lost it."

"Be quiet."

"It'll turn up Dave. I'll have a look for it when I've done the bedrooms."

Dave grumbled his way through breakfast and he was still muttering curses on whoever had moved his watch as he set out for work.

Only on Thursdays were the children let off their chores

- making their own beds and tidying their bedrooms before they went to school. Thursday was the day Hilda 'did' the bedrooms. It was always the same routine. Change the bedding, dust each bedroom in turn, then vacuum through to the landing and down the stairs. She had already changed the bedding on Blanche's and Paul's beds. Sam's was next. She was busy stripping his bed when she noticed something glinting as it caught the sunlight on his bedside table. She gasped, disbelieving her own eyes at first. It was. There on top of the book he was reading was Dave's watch. Hilda picked it up and listened . It was ticking and didn't seem damaged so why had he brought it upstairs? It didn't make sense. He knew she'd find it. Why? What reason did he have? All morning she pondered on it. Dave had hardly got through the door that evening when she told him of her find.

"Why on earth should he steal my watch? He's been here over two years now and never done anything like this," he shook his head. "Well, not that we know of. You haven't missed anything before, have you?"

"No, of course not. And I don't think he meant to steal it. It was there in full view. He'd made no attempt to hide it, and leaving it there he knew I couldn't help but see it. It's all so stupid."

"Have you said anything to him?"

" No. I didn't know what to say."

"Did he seem any different at teatime? I thought he seemed a lot happier lately, did you?"

Hilda nodded, "I don't understand it at all. I really don't."

"When he comes in I'll have a word with him."

"Be careful what you say, Dave, you know how sensitive he is."

Dave glanced up at his wife in surprise. That was a new one, he thought. Suddenly she's defending the lad.

"Tact, my dear, is my middle name."

Hilda snorted.

It was only a few minutes later that the front door slammed and they heard Sam's voice say, "It's only me, Aunty Hilda."

"Sam!"

"Yes, Uncle Dave." Sam poked his head round the door.

"Come here a minute, will you?" Dave led the way into the front room.

"Summat up?"

"That's what I want to find out."

Sam lifted his eyebrows. "Sounds serious."

Dave remembered Hilda's warning and tempered his reply with, "I hope not, Sam. I found my watch."

"Oh, great! Where was it?"

"That's just what I want to talk to you about. It was in your bedroom."

"What?"

"On your bedside table."

"How'd it get there?"

"That's what I want to know."

"Come on, Uncle Dave, why should I take your watch upstairs to my bedroom? I never touched it, honest."

"I can't understand it either, Sam, but your Aunty Hilda found it when she was making the beds."

Sam shook his head in dismay. "You're not saying…."

Quickly Dave interrupted. "No, I'm not. Don't think that, Sam. I just can't fathom out how it got there, that's all."

"Well, it wasn't my doing." Sam was getting annoyed.

"OK. Let's forget it, shall we. Come on, we'll go and watch the tele."

"I'm going out," and Sam slammed the door behind him

Dave went disconsolately back to the kitchen where Hilda sat waiting. She had heard rather than seen Sam go out and knew there could have been no simple explanation of how the watch had suddenly appeared in his bedroom.

"I told you to be tactful."

"I was."

"He was upset. Anyway, what did he have to say about it?"

"Denied ever touching the watch."

Hilda shook her head sadly, "It's beyond me."

The following Wednesday evening Dave and Hilda had planned a night out at their local. Hilda, dressed up and looking glamorous, with her hair newly washed and set, was searching through her jewellery box.

"That's funny," she turned to Dave who was making heavy weather of tying his tie, "I can only find one of my earrings."

"Well, wear that," Dave said absentmindedly.

"You're not listening. I've lost one of those pearl earrings you bought me for our anniversary."

"When did you last wear them?" Dave was serious now. Those earrings had cost him a fortune and for Hilda to lose one so soon after he'd given them to her rankled.

"It was last Christmas, when we went to Vera's."

"Ask her to have a look for it then."

"She'd have found it by now if I'd left it there. She knows what they're like and that they're mine because she tried them on." Dave rubbed his knuckles across his lips, a sure sign he was annoyed but Hilda hadn't finished, "Besides, I remember taking them off and putting them away when we got home."

"Let me have a look," Dave took several pieces of jewellery from the box and laid them on the dressing table top. "Here it is," triumphantly he picked up the earring from amongst the other jewellery.

"That's the other one, you idiot." they were both annoyed now.

"If that's your attitude, look for it yourself." and Dave stalked out of the room.

Hilda sat on the bed fuming. Fat lot of help Dave was in a crisis and she felt this really was a crisis. Her pearl earrings were her pride and joy. She'd never had anything as expensive in her life and now one was missing. She started to look once again, going through all the drawers in the dressing table, even looking through Dave's things though she knew it was pointless. Wasn't that just her luck. Nothing ever seemed to go right for her. She shed a few tears. Even Dave had lost his temper with her. That was it, then. Her evening was ruined.

"Ready yet?" Dave poked his head round the door but when he saw she was crying he came into the room and put his arms round her. "Sorry, love. I shouldn't have said that."

"I'm sorry too Dave but I'm so upset about losing it."

Dave kissed the top of her head and grinned, "I'll have to see about getting you another pair for our silver wedding."

Hilda giggled, "That's ages away. Ten years I'll have to wait. "

Serious now, Dave said, "It'll turn up, love, don't worry. So," he lifted her to her feet, " are we going out or not?"

"I don't feel like going anywhere now."

"Come on, love. It'll take your mind off it."

"I'll just go and ask the children if they've seen it, then."

Dave took hold of her arm, "Not now. Let's go. They're all watching the tele. You'll never get 'em to listen."

...

At breakfast that Thursday morning Hilda broached the subject of the missing earring. "..it's special, you see, or I wouldn't bother about it."

"What's it like?" Sam asked. "Mmh, nice, but I haven't seen it." he said, when Hilda showed him the mate to the one she'd lost.

"Neither have I," Paul said.

Blanche merely shook her head.

Hilda sighed, "Keep a lookout for it, will you?"

When the children had gone to school Hilda got out the vacuum cleaner but without the usual enthusiasm she had for housework, dragging herself through the usual routine of changing the bedding and dusting, first Blanche's room, then Paul's, followed by Sam's, the last bedroom to receive her attention being her own and Dave's. It was when she lifted the pillow in Sam's bedroom that she saw it. The shock forced her to sit down with a thump on the bed. She picked up the earring and held it in the palm of her hand, looking at it without really seeing it. Her head was spinning. She kept saying aloud, "Sam. Sam. What have you done?" Why, she wondered, would he take just one earring? What was the point of it? He couldn't sell it, and like Dave's watch he must have known she would find it. It just didn't make sense. Surely he wasn't trying to hurt her. So why? Unless...the thought that came shocked her more than thinking he'd deliberately stolen it... he couldn't help it!!! He'd had a blackout - a fit of some kind. After all, his mother was unstable. But his mother didn't have fits, not until they gave her those drugs, still... She got to her feet. There was no use speculating. She'd put it to Dave, see what he thought. The rest of the day dragged on interminably.

Dave, when she told him, repeated what she had said to herself that morning. "Why would he take just one earring? He knew you'd find it anyway, leaving it under his pillow. It just doesn't make sense."

Then Hilda put to him her thoughts on Sam's mental health. For a long time he looked at her, then he said, "Oh, God! I hope not. Please, God, don't let it be that. After all, his mother.."

"No. I thought about that. Amy doesn't have fits. It's not the same. At least, I hope not. He's not autistic, far from it. All afternoon I've been going over and over it and I've come to the conclusion that it's the reaction to all the trouble he's had plus the fact that he's been working so hard at school. You heard Mr Fenwick say what a hard working lad he was. 'Grammar School material' is how he put it."

"You could have a point I suppose, but it's over two years since he came to us and besides…." Dave had been going to say that Paul had worked hard too without any ill effects but of course Paul hadn't had, as Hilda said, the trauma of losing his home and his mother. " It could be delayed reaction I suppose. Perhaps we should take him to see Dr Reynolds."

"He won't go."

"He will." Dave said with conviction.

Dave waited until he knew Paul and Blanche were out for the evening before he spoke to Sam about finding the earring. He knew what he had to say wouldn't be easy and he didn't want either Paul or Blanche barging in on their conversation. He had to admit to himself that he wasn't the most tactful of men and he knew too that Sam was as touchy as hell sometimes.

"So," Dave leaned back in his chair, "how was school today, Sam?" he felt this was a stupid way to start the conversation but he could think of no other opening gambit.

"OK." Sam looked at his uncle a might warily.

"You have exams coming up soon, haven't you?" Sam nodded. "Are you finding it hard going. I know I did. I hated exams."

"I don't feel too bad about it. I like maths. It's just my spelling that let's me down. Mr Fenwick says I'm a bit dyslexic."

"Dis what?"

"Word blind. But I'm coping."

Here the conversation stalled while Dave desperately tried to think of a way to bring up the subject of the missing earring. Fortunately for Dave it was Sam who mentioned it.

"Has Aunty Hilda found her earring?"

"As a matter of fact she has, Sam."

"Good. That's great. She told us it was special. Where was it?"

"Under your pillow." Dave hadn't meant to make such a bald statement but now it was said he watched Sam's reaction closely.

Sam turned pale and shook his head as if to rid himself of his thoughts, "I don't get it, Uncle Dave. Why would it be under my pillow? I never touched her earring, in fact I never saw them before she showed us this morning, honest. Why would I do that to Aunty Hilda, anyway? It's not fair. I wouldn't. I wouldn't." Sam's voice got louder and shriller with every word.

"Now, then, Sam." Dave put his hand on the boy's shoulder realising that he was getting hysterical, "Calm down. Nobody thinks you meant to take it, Sam, but we, your Aunty Hilda and me that is, think…" Dave sought a tactful explanation.

"Think what?"

"We think you might have taken that earring and my watch without knowing what you were doing. Sort of sleep walking."

"No! No! You're trying to say I'm going barmy, like my Mam."

"I'm NOT. Your Mam's, well.. she's just a bit slow,

like - autistic they say. It's entirely different."

"Different from me, you mean. I'm the barmy one."

"No, of course not. We just think maybe you've been working too hard for these exams and on top of everything else, well..." Dave spread his hands, at a loss for words. "Sam," again Dave put his hand on Sam's shoulder, "we want you to go and see Dr Reynolds. He'll make an appointment to see a specialist if he thinks you need one."

"See a shrink, you mean. Oh, no! They'll put me away."

"Nobody's going to put you anywhere. We wouldn't let them. No, Sam, all they'll do is give you some pills to take for a while. Trust me lad. I won't let them do anything you don't want."

"What's the alternative?"

"There isn't one."

Sam shrugged. He was deathly pale and his eyes were troubled.

"Come on now. There's nothing to worry about. It's better than living under a cloud like we are doing at present."

Sam's visit to Dr. Reynolds resulted in an appointment being made to see the psychiatrist a month later. The strain on Sam was all but unbearable and he wished the interview over and done with. Paul was his mainstay during those black days, "Don't worry, kid, there's nothing wrong with you. There's got to be an explanation for all this stupid business but I can't think what. I'm working on it though."

Blanche on the other hand, had a triumphant gleam in her eye, "Will they take him away, Mam? He can go and live at that hospital with his Mam."

"That's enough of that sort of talk, young lady. Sam's family, remember. It's just that he's got run down, that's all. He's had a lot to contend with lately. They'll give him some medicine and that'll soon put him right,"

Under her breath Blanche muttered, "Pity."

"What did you say?"

"Nothing, Mam."

...

"Our Paul's got a girlfriend," Blanche announced to the rest of the family over their evening meal.

Paul's face reddened, "Big mouth."

"Is that right?" Dave grinned at his son.

"She's just a friend."

Sam nudged Paul, "Some friend."

Hilda smiled benignly and said, "That's nice, love. What's she called?"

His sister gave Paul a coy look, "She's called Eunice and she's given him a present."

"How d'you know?"

"Her sister told me. She's in my class at school."

"A present, eh?" Dave looked expectantly at his son.

"OK, then. She gave me a wallet." taking it from his pocket Paul passed it over to his father.

"Anything in it?" Dave opened the flap to look inside.

"Not yet. I haven't any money."

"No, 'cos he bought her a bracelet."

Paul muttered threats at his sister, while Dave, still in a teasing mood said, "Did he, by gum?"

"Leave him alone, Dave. That's very nice, Paul," and Hilda handed the wallet back. Her son slipped it into his pocket. "You'll have to bring Eunice to tea one day."

Paul glanced at his watch, eager to get away from this inquisition. "I'm off. See you!" he called as he disappeared through the front door.

"So," Dave leaned back in his chair exuding an air of satisfaction, "he's got a girlfriend, has he? What about you then, Sam? Have you got a girl?"

"Not me." Sam shook his head, "I keep away from women."

Blanche snorted. Hilda giggled. Dave laughed aloud and said. "Very wise, my lad."

...

When Paul got home that night he went straight upstairs to his bedroom, took off his blazer and put it on the chair next to his bed then went into the bathroom before going downstairs for his supper. Only Blanche and Sam sat at the table.

"Where's Mam and Dad,"

Sam shrugged, "Dunno."

"They've gone to help old Mrs Bradley with something or other. Where've you been anyway? Been out with Eunice, have you?" Blanche asked.

"What's it to do with you, blabber mouth?" Paul was still annoyed that she had told their parents about Eunice. That had been his secret. Something he had wanted to keep to himself at least for a little while longer. He had a sudden impulse to slap her. She saw the signs, "I'm going to bed."

"Good riddance."

At the door she turned and pulled her tongue out at them.

"One of these days I'll murder that sister of mine."

Sam said nothing - just hoped it would be soon.

Paul woke next morning and lay thinking about Eunice. He said her name softly to himself and it sent the blood racing through his veins. He smiled broadly. Leaning out of bed he felt in his blazer pocket for the wallet. It wasn't there. A rush of anger jolted him out of bed. He felt sure it had been there when he got home; he remembered feeling for it as he came in last night. He'd come straight upstairs to his room, hadn't he? He'd put his blazer on the chair back before he'd gone downstairs. After that he couldn't remember whether he'd touched his blazer again or not. Perhaps the wallet had fallen on the floor. Vainly Paul searched under the chair, under the bed, under the dressing table but without luck. He let out a breath of despair. How could he tell Eunice he'd lost her present so soon after she'd given it to him But he hadn't lost it. He knew it had been in his pocket when he came in. He couldn't let it go like that. It must be somewhere in the house. Paul tried to remember who had been around after he'd come home. His eyes narrowed. So that was the game, was it? He waited until Sam had gone downstairs for his breakfast then went into his cousin's room, looked under the pillow and in the dressing table drawers, plus one or two other places his wallet might be hidden, then, satisfied that it wasn't there he followed Sam into the kitchen.

"Hi!" Sam said, with his mouth full of toast as usual. Paul didn't answer. "What's up Paul? You mad at me or something?"

Paul shook his head. "I don't want any breakfast, Mam."

"Why, what's the matter, Paul?"

"Nothing."

Hilda sighed. Was it worth it, she thought, what love did to you?

Blanche wriggled out of her chair, "Can I go now, Mam?"

"Wash your sticky hands before you do, love." Hilda gave her daughter a kiss.

"I'm going to." and she ran upstairs followed a second later by Paul.

Suddenly the upstairs landing erupted in a screaming, yelling fight.

"I thought you had something to do with it," Paul's voice came down to them high with rage, "you evil little bitch."

Hilda, with Sam close behind, raced up the stairs to find Paul shaking his sister violently by the shoulders.

"Paul!" his mother screamed above the row, "Stop it. Right now. What's going on? What's this all about?"

"This," Paul said, holding Blanche by the scruff of the neck, "is your thief." he was red in the face with anger, "Just look in Sam's room, Mam, and you'll find my wallet. She thought we'd blame Sam again, that's why she put it there. That's what she did with Dad's watch and your earring."

"I didn't, Mam, I didn't."

"You liar," Paul lifted his hand to slap her but his mother intercepted the blow.

"I won't have that, Paul. I think you had better explain yourself. If your wallet is in Sam's room then he must have put it there."

"No, I didn't. I never touched it." Sam wailed.

"No, he's right, Mam. He never touched my wallet. I

missed it this morning. I looked all over my bedroom for it but it wasn't there so I waited until I heard Sam go downstairs then I searched his room. Sorry, Sam, but I had to make sure. There was no wallet and Sam hasn't been upstairs until now but madam has, I caught her coming out of Sam's room and I bet you you'll find my wallet there."

Hilda pushed passed them into Sam's bedroom. Under the pillow was Paul's wallet. She turned with it in her hand and looking down at her daughter said, "What's all this about, Blanche? You'd better have a good explanation because otherwise I hate to think what your father will do when I tell him."

Blanche lifted her chin defiantly and looked at Sam. "I hate him. I never wanted him here in the first place. You and Dad love him more than me and it's not fair. I want him to go away. I want us to be like we were before."

The other three seemed turned to stone at this outburst. Sam's face was ashen. He stared back at Blanche for a second or two then he turned, went downstairs and out through the door. It all seemed to happen in slow motion; then Hilda came to life, "Go after him, Paul."

But when Paul reached the gate there was no sign of Sam. There was no sign of him at school either. Paul wasn't sure what to do. Perhaps Sam wanted to be alone. He usually did when there was any trouble. He'd be home for his dinner, Paul assured himself.

CHAPTER 6

When Sam left the house he knew exactly what he was going to do. He made straight for the hospital and his mother. The big heavy door of the hospital was closed and locked when he got there but one of the maids answered to his knock.

"I want to see me Mam," he pushed past the girl and made for his mother's room.

"Sammy!" she held out her arms to him as she usually did, "Sammy, love, you're early."

"Mam," he buried his head on her shoulder and burst into tears; tears that had needed to be shed for so long.

"Oh! don't cry, Sammy, don't cry."

Sam dried his eyes and shook his head. "Mam, will you tell me something. When I've asked you before you wouldn't but now I have to know."

"Know what, love?"

"Who my father is."

Amy's mouth shut tight. Sam wasn't sure whether she'd understood until he saw the anxious look in her eyes.

"Please Mam. I can't go back to Uncle Dave's, they don't want me and I don't know where to go or what to do. I thought, if I could talk to my father he'd help me."

Amy didn't answer, she just looked down at her fingers twisting together on her lap.

"Mam?"

Amy shook her head.

"Don't you know, Mam"?

Amy nodded now, still not looking at him.

"Well?"

"He made me promise."

"Who made you promise, Mam?"

"Old Mr Wilmott. He told your Gran he'd want the money back if we told anybody and we'd spent it, you see. Your Gran paid off what we owed as soon as we got it."

Sam didn't understand any of this but he had to know, it was vital to him to find his father because he knew he couldn't go back there and he had no one else to turn to.

"Mam, I've got to know. If you love me, tell me. I won't say you've told me, I promise but PLEASE, PLEASE, tell me his name. Tell me what he's like."

"He's nice, Sammy. Handsome." she nodded to confirm this statement. "Very handsome, like you, Sammy."

"Did he ever come to see me?"

Amy shook her head.

Sam looked at his mother now and tears started in his eyes again There was no point in asking her any more questions, he felt she didn't understand how important this was to him. He sat beside her on her bed, his head down the tears wet on his cheek. Gently Amy took hold of his hand. "His name is Roger Wilmott."

Sam stared at his mother. So she had understood. He threw his arms around her and kissed her cheek. "Thanks, Mam. I love you."

It wasn't much to go on, just a name. Sam wasn't sure where to start and there was nobody he could ask. He couldn't go up to some complete stranger and say 'Do you know where Roger Wilmott lives?' now could he? No, he couldn't do that but, - the idea came to him as he passed the public telephone in the hospital foyer - there was the telephone directory. He fingered through the pages until he came to the Wilmots. Some of the names were spelt with one 't', some with two 'tts', some with one 'l', some with two 'lls' .Sam ran his finger down the page and felt his hand shake as he read, 'Roger Wilmott, The Garth, Westford Rise.' Now what? He started to dial the number in the phone book, put the receiver down, his courage drained. Then he thought about the alternative - going back to Uncle Dave's. He redialled, listened to the 'phone ringing at the other end and almost put the receiver down again. He was scared, he had to admit it. How would his father react to him turning up like this? "Dammit!" he said aloud. What had he to be scared of. This man had neglected him and his Mam for more than ten years. It was this Roger Wilmott who should be scared because when he saw him he was going to give him a piece of his mind - well, if he wouldn't help him, that is. The 'phone stopped ringing and a female voice said, "Hello, Mr Wilmott's residence."

"I want to speak to Mr Roger Wilmott."

"I'm afraid Mr Wilmott's at a Council meeting this morning."

"Can you tell me when he'll be in, or could you give me his office number?"

"I don't know when he'll be back, and as to his office number, it depends what you want. I'm only his housekeeper, I can't pass on information about Mr Wilmott over the telephone."

"It's a personal matter." Sam thought that sounded important.

"Perhaps you could call back later or give me your number and I'll leave a note for him to call you."

Before Sam could answer his money ran out. He counted the change in his pocket and decided he couldn't afford to ring back now. He looked at the telephone for a minute, then it dawned on him; of course, the woman had told him where his father was. He was at a Council Meeting. That meant he was in the Town Hall. What an idiot he was not to have realised that before.

By the time Sam reached the Town Hall it was almost mid-day. A few men in dark suits were drifting out of the Committee Room. One or two of them looked askance at the boy wandering around the corridors in his school uniform. Sam slowed his steps as another group filed out, amongst them a face Sam recognised. He'd seen the man quite often passing the school as the children came out at lunch time. Sam surmised he must live nearby. The man looked at him now, obviously in his turn recognising him. Sam was about to ask him if he knew where Mr Wilmott might be when someone called, "Councillor Wilmott!" The man turned in response and Sam's heart missed a beat. *So this was his father.* For a second Roger Wilmott hesitated then he motioned Sam to wait.

While he stood waiting Sam studied the man carefully. He was tall, with hair almost as fair as his own. If he had been asked to describe Roger Wilmott Sam would have said 'he was a bit posh'. Roger certainly had an air of confidence; of being self assured and this was something

Sam couldn't help but have a sneaking admiration for, yet he told himself that this man's treatment of him gave him no reason to admire anything about him. His mother had said he was handsome. Sam didn't know about that. His Gran used to say 'Handsome is as handsome does.' If that was so then this man should be ugly and cruel to abandon him and his mother when they needed him most but he didn't look cruel Sam had to admit. This was the man he'd so often tried to imagine, a man he needed desperately now.

"Look, I've something urgent on at the moment," he heard his father saying, "I'll 'phone you later," then he turned to Sam.

That'll be it, Sam thought, he'll say he's too busy. Well, he's not going to get away with it that easy. He set his face and braced himself for the battle of wills he expected.

"Come on," Roger put a hand on Sam's shoulder and steered him towards a small office marked 'Private'. "we can talk in here." He perched himself on the edge of the desk and indicated a chair for Sam. "So," he lifted his eyebrows, "young Sam. You've come to me at last."

It was a remark that totally disarmed his son. Sam had come in search of this man, his belly full of hatred and hot words burning to be said. How was he going to spew out the venomous speech he had prepared now? How could he answer this man who sat smiling at him? He had expected denials and evasions. He had been prepared to shout above the man's rejection of him. Prepared to force him to listen to the trail of misery his meanness had caused and to throw into his face the fact that all his life he had been dubbed a bastard because of him. 'Well, I'm *your* bastard' he had been going to say. But now, with his father's unqualified acceptance of him he was left speechless, so he just nodded.

"Your mother told you about me, I take it."

For the first time Sam spoke, his voice hoarse with the anger he suppressed. "Yes, she told me but only because I made her." he found himself on the defensive and he was annoyed, "She said I hadn't to cause any trouble and I promised, but I don't know why, after all…."

"Whoa! Whoa!" Roger held up his hand, "Look, Sam, I'm glad you've come. I've wanted to get to know you. Don't imagine I've never thought about you. I'd have made myself known to you before now but I wasn't sure how you'd react. Now if there's any way I can help you, I will. Obviously there is or you wouldn't be here now." he looked at his watch, "so, if it's a long story why don't we go and have a bite to eat while you tell me what it's all about?" he stood up, "I'm hungry and I bet you are too, aren't you, Sam?"

Sam could only nod.

The restaurant was across the road from the Town Hall, a new building with wide windows Inside it was spacious with tables set well apart, tables with gleaming white cloths set with polished cutlery and sparkling glasses. The waiter inclined his head in recognition of Roger's greeting. and took them to a table in the window.

"What is it to be today, Mr Wilmott." he included Sam in this and handed him a menu.

"Well, Sam, what would you like to eat?"

"Wait a bit. I can't decide," Sam's eyes goggled, not just at the choice but at the prices.

"The steak pie is delicious, sir. I can recommend it."

Sam had never been called 'sir' before. He liked it. He frowned now at the menu in an effort to appear accustomed to eating out, then he nodded. "Yes, the steak pie sounds very nice. I'll have that."

"New potatoes or chips, sir?"

"Chips, yes, chips and peas, please."

Roger Wilmott watched his son with an amused smiled tugging at the corners of his mouth and thought, yes, I can make something of this young man.

"I'll have the same, Toni, and two glasses of fruit juice to start. We'll order pudding later."

Toni gave a slight bow and departed.

"Now then, perhaps you'll tell me what's bothering you, Sam. It's nothing to do with the police, is it?"

Sam wagged his head, "No. Nothing like that..." he hesitated to give this man a title. Mr Wilmott seemed too formal and yet, Dad, at this point didn't seem right either.

Roger noticed the hesitation, "If you don't want to call me Dad you can call me Roger, OK?"

Sam blinked and gave a quick nod. This chap wasn't so bad after all. But then he remembered those years after his Gran died when there was little to eat in the house and he frowned not quite knowing how or where to start. His Gran always said start at the beginning so he took a deep breath and said, "They came and took our furniture away." there was that 'they' again, but he had no other name for them, "and they sent my Mam to the.." feeling brutal he said, "loony bin. But she's not mad. The doctor said she is autistic. Uncle Dave said it was because she couldn't look after herself properly let alone me. So then I had to go and live with him and Aunty Hilda but they don't want me.

Uncle Dave's OK, and Paul's my best mate but Aunty Hilda and Blanche hate me."

"It must be tough having to live with someone who doesn't like you. Do you like them?"

"I like Paul and , like I said, Uncle Dave's OK. I didn't like Aunty Hilda at first 'cos she threatened to put me in an orphanage."

"What had you done?"

"I was upset when I saw the men taking our things out of number twelve, that's where Mam and me lived, so I went to my hideout and....well, I fell asleep. It was five o'clock when I woke up and they were all mad at me 'cos I'd not been back for my dinner." Roger nodded understandingly. "After you sent the money - it was you, wasn't it?" Sam didn't wait for an answer, "she was a lot nicer to me. I think she'd been worried 'cos Uncle Dave couldn't do any overtime and they were short of money." Sam looked at his father now and wondered if he understood what it was like being short of money. When Roger said nothing he went on, "Blanche was a bitch but I couldn't hit her - she's a girl."

"Of course not."

"Only this time," he said with an old fashioned nod of his head, "she's gone too far."

Roger coughed into his handkerchief, then he said, "In what way has she gone too far, Sam?"

"She tried to frame me, didn't she?" this phrase he'd learned from a recent gangster film he'd seen on the television and thought it fitted the situation very well. "She pinched Uncle Dave's watch and put it in my room, then another time she took Aunty Hilda's earring and put it under my pillow."

"She did what?" Roger's voice rose in disbelief.

"She knew that Aunty Hilda would find these things and they'd think that I was the thief." Sam paled at the memory. "They were going to send me to a psy.... shrink and get me put in a loony bin like Mam."

"They really thought you'd stolen these things?"

Sam nodded, "They said I must have been sleep walking when I did it."

"Do you know for sure it was Blanche?"

"Don't you believe me either?"

"Of course I do but it could have been Paul."

Sam shook his head. "It was Paul who caught her at it. She was putting his new wallet under my pillow so they'd blame me for that too but Paul suspected her all along. When she went upstairs after he'd missed his wallet, he followed her and saw her coming out of my bedroom. There was a heck of a row. Paul shook her like a jelly but Aunty Hilda stopped him. She didn't 'alf tell Blanche off though. Blanche said she'd done it 'cos she hated me and wanted me out of the house."

"What did Dave say?"

"I didn't wait to find out. I scarpered."

Roger took a deep breath but before he could make any comment Sam said, "I'm not going back there. That's why I came to see if you would tell me what to do."

"That's a poser, isn't it Sam?"

The waiter brought their meal at this point and at first Sam just toyed with the food until his father said, "Don't worry, son, we'll sort something out. I'd take you home with me but there's a problem. You see, my wife died a few months back and so I'm on my own. When I go abroad on business there'd be nobody to look after you."

"Haven't you got any kids? I could stay with them."

"Only one - you."

"I can look after myself."

"I'm sure you can, Sam, only, well, it wouldn't be right, would it? But don't worry, as I said, we'll sort something out."

"When you go abroad, couldn't I go with you?"

"You can when you're older, Sam but right now there's your education to think about. How would you like to go to a public school?"

The idea didn't appeal to Sam. He'd heard about these places. They sounded like the orphanage he'd been so desperate to keep away from. Visions of that huge dormitory and the harsh regime returned. He shook his head, "Don't fancy that, besides it costs a lot of money, doesn't it?"

"I can afford it. I have my own engineering works."

"You own it?"

"My father built up the business and when he died I inherited it."

"Mam said you were a manager."

"So I was. My father was the big boss then. Now I'm the boss."

Sam's eyes narrowed. "Then why did Mam and me go hungry? Why didn't you give us some help, then?"

"I did, Sam," Roger looked hurt and surprised. "I gave you enough to live on. Where did it go? Did your mother gamble?"

"No, she didn't."

"Then what happened to the money?"

"Dunno."

"So that's why Dave asked me for money," Roger said half to himself, "I thought he was on the scrounge."

"Aunty Hilda spent all that money you sent buying me new clothes. Uncle Dave just gave me five pounds of it."

Roger was thoughtful for a moment, then said "I wonder." Sam looked at him askance. "I think we should go across to the bank next, Sam, to see what's happened to all those cheques I paid in to your account."

"My account?" Sam's eyes boggled. He had an account in the bank.!

"Yours and your mother's."

"Good afternoon, Mr Wilmott," the bank manager shook Roger's hand and showed them into his office. "Now, what can I do for you, sir?"

There it was again 'sir'. Sam liked the sound of it.

Roger was speaking, "Sam here has an account with you, a joint account with his mother Amy Watson, and we would like to know what the balance is."

The man hesitated, "Er…we do need proof of identification, Councillor, you understand."

"Sam is my son, Mr March. Is that good enough for you?"

The pause that followed this was almost imperceptible. If the man was shocked by this revelation he didn't let it show. He nodded his head, "Yes, of course, Mr Wilmott, of course." He pressed a button on his desk, "I'll see to it immediately," he said and made a note on his pad. In answer to his ring a young woman appeared. "Get me details of this account will you Julie, please," and he handed her the note he'd written.

"Yes, Mr Marsh," she said and retreated through the door.

"A fine boy," the bank manager said by way of passing the time.

"He's got potential," Roger winked at his son.

Sam kicked his heels in embarrassment. He found it humiliating to be discussed as if he were some inanimate object, so it was a relief when the young woman came back with the information they needed.

"Here we are, Councillor." Mr Marsh rustled the slip of paper he'd been given. "Now let me see. The balance to date is £1,567 exactly and with the balance accrued over the past year that will make a total of £1,724. 10.6d. Sam's head whirled. He swallowed hard and looked across at his father but Roger's face was impassive. "There appear to have been no withdrawals for the last two years," the man said, in answer to Roger's question. The only signature we have is that of Amy Watson."

Roger nodded, "Just as I thought," then turning to Sam he asked, "Was that about the time your Gran died?"

Sam said he thought so, "Gran used to bring Mam to the bank every week." he told them.

"Sam's mother, Amy Watson, is… incapacitated, I'm afraid, so you'll need a specimen signature from Sam, presumably. That way he can have access to his money."

"That's right." Mr Marsh smiled across as Sam, "We can easily arrange that, sir." 'sir' again. Sam was beginning to enjoy this, although he felt this time it didn't have quite the same ring as when the waiter said it. "If you will just sign this form" and the manager took a printed sheet of paper from the drawer in his desk, "here," he indicated a dotted line on the page, "and again, here. Good. Good. Now Councillor, if you would sign as witness." Roger signed his name with a flourish, "Thank you. That is all that's necessary."

Outside on the pavement Sam felt decidedly shaky.

"I could buy my own house with all that money."

"I'd rather you used it towards your education, young man. I don't want to find you've spent the lot on something daft."

"I won't."

"Best keep it to yourself too. You'll find yourself very popular if you spread it around that you have a bit of money, until it's all gone, that is. Then all your friends will disappear, together with the money."

Roger's tone lightened, " I want you to listen carefully to what I say now. I shall still pay in the monthly cheque and you can give your Uncle Dave enough for your keep. See what they think is a fair amount and give them that every week. I can trust you to do that, can't I, Sam?"

"I told you, I'm not going back there."

"Well, we'll see. Now I suppose I'd better 'phone your Aunty.. What's she called…?"

"Hilda."

"Hilda, and let her know that you're safe. They've probably dragged the canal for you by now."

Sam smirked, "Doubt it. Anyway, they're not on the 'phone."

"I'll have to go round there then. What'll you do while

I'm gone?"

"Dunno."

"Tell you what. Come with me."

"No. I told you."

"You can sit outside in the car."

Sam didn't want to go, neither did he want to be left alone.

"Well?"

"OK, but I'm not going in the house. I'll keep my head down so they can't see me."

"Please yourself." Roger grinned.

...

The pleasantly plump woman who answered the door to Roger's knock had an anxious look.

"Mrs Watson?"

"Yes."

"I'm Roger Wilmott."

"Yes, I know who you are."

"May I come in for a moment?"

Hilda nodded and stood aside while Roger stepped inside the hall but she left the front door open knowing Dave would object to her asking Roger Wilmott's into their house.

"I've come…"

"You'd better know…"

They both spoke at once.

"Sorry," Roger waved a hand, "after you."

"I was going to say, Sam's disappeared - run off again. We had a bit of trouble this morning…"

Dave strode into the hall, "What's this then? You should know you're not welcome in this house, Wilmott."

"You do know who I am, then." Roger's voice was heavy with sarcasm. "I thought, when you came asking for money, you weren't aware that I was Sam's father."

Dave flushed at the implication that he'd been on the scrounge. "Yes, I know he's your son and you've a right to support him."

"Look," Hilda broke in after seeing the curtains twitching across the road, "Can't we have this conversation inside."

Roger followed Hilda and Dave into the kitchen, saying as he went, "I have, all along. I only discovered today that Amy hasn't been drawing on the money for the last two years - money I paid into her account."

"What money?"

"The cheque I pay in every month. Anyway I haven't come to discuss money. I've come to tell you that Sam's alright. That's if you're interested, of course."

This bit of sarcasm wasn't lost in Hilda. "Of course we are. Where is he?" she grabbed Roger's sleeve in her agitation. "For heaven's sake, if you know where he is, tell us."

"Sam's in my car," he thumbed in the direction of the vehicle standing at the kerb. "But he won't come in. He says he's not coming back here, and from what he told me today I don't blame him."

"In your car? Is he alright?" Dave made towards the door.

"Leave it a minute," Roger said angrily. "We have to talk."

Dave, somewhat mollified at the knowledge that Roger had supported Sam, asked him to sit down, then said

"Well?"

"He came looking for me. Evidently he'd been to see Amy. She told him who I was and I'm glad she did. I've wanted to get to know my son for a long time now but I didn't know how he would react. Anyway, Sam and I had a long talk. It's cleared up a lot of misunderstandings for both of us."

"Not before time either, " Dave eyed his visitor with distaste.

"I'm not particularly bothered how you judge me but I want Sam to know that I'm not proud of what happened."

"You were married. You had no right to seduce my sister."

"Yes, I was married. Unhappily married. You wouldn't know what it's like to live with a woman who has no love, no feelings for you."

"Oh, spare me for heaven's sake. All this sob stuff doesn't excuse what you did."

"Maybe not but I never forced Amy to do anything against her will."

"Amy didn't have a will of her own you must have known that."

"No, I don't accept that. She was a very beautiful young woman. Naive maybe, but as regards sex she was very experienced."

"That's a lie."

"I wasn't the first by a long chalk. You can ask anybody - Ralph Haines, for a start, John Williams or Charlie Blake - ask them. They were friends of yours, weren't they? You ask them about your sister."

"You bastard!" Dave sprang from his chair with every

intention of venting his anger on some part, any part, of Roger Wilmott but Hilda held him back.

"Stop it Dave. It's true. Everybody knew she was man mad. Everybody but you it seems."

Roger looked disparagingly at Dave, "Hitting me won't help matters, you know. Anyway, don't imagine I can't defend myself. This attitude of yours isn't getting us anywhere, is it?. If you'd just listen for a minute; just put yourself in my place perhaps you'll see things differently." Roger held up his hand when Dave tried to interrupt. "When Amy told me she was pregnant I wasn't sure it was my child. On the other hand I couldn't risk the scandal so I took responsibility for it, or rather my father did on condition that my name wasn't brought into it. That wasn't my idea, I loved Amy and I love kids. My wife and I never had any, so whether he's mine or not I don't care, I'm going to look after his welfare. What happens next depends on you and Sam. I can't take him in because I have to travel abroad quite a bit and it wouldn't be right to leave him alone in the house, he's not old enough yet. But Sam says he's not coming back to you. He says you don't want him."

"But we do. We do." Hilda was almost in tears.

"Well then, it's up to Sam. I've offered to pay for him to go to a Public School but he won't. So what's the alternative?"

Dave shook his head slowly from side to side. "It's a problem. Of course he can come back here. He's our flesh and blood but after what's happened I'm not surprised he feels as he does. Our Blanche has been a little bitch to that lad. I'm ashamed of her. She says she's sorry." Dave paused and shook his head once more. "It was jealousy that made her do what she did. She felt we were making more of Sam than her."

"That's not true, of course," Hilda cut in, "It was just that he was in such a state when they took Amy away. Turned them out on the street, they did. Where were you then, Mr Wilmott?"

"There was nothing I could do. It was the Welfare Department's problem. Their report said Amy was incapable of looking after the boy. I went to look at the house and had to agree. Did you see the state it was in. But you must have."

Dave hung his head, "Aye, we tried to help but she just couldn't cope. She was getting worse all the time and Sam was running wild. To be honest I don't think they could have done anything else."

"So what's to be done now?"

"I think we'd better talk to him."

"Right! Let's see if we can get him to come in." Roger got up and went out to his car only to find Sam wasn't there. "He's gone," he called over his shoulder.

"Bloody hell! Where do we go from here?" Dave's sigh came from deep inside him, "We'll have to start looking for him all over again. One thing's certain, he won't have gone back to number twelve. There's somebody else living there now."

"I'll 'phone the hospital," Roger volunteered, "Maybe he's gone back to see his mother," and he took off down the road to the 'phone box on the corner while Dave made for the school, though he had little hope of finding Sam there now that the other children had gone home.

"Mam!" Blanche tugged at her mother's sleeve. "Mam, it's all my fault. Let me go and find him and I'll tell him I'm sorry." Now that she realised the enormity of what she had done Blanche felt she had to make some effort to make amends.

"Where else can you look, Blanche?"

"He goes to the park when he's in trouble. There's a tree he sits under, a willow tree, and you can't see him unless you get close. I'll go there."

"Alright, But be careful, Blanche, and don't hang about there too long. There's some funny folk go in there after dark. If you see our Paul get him to go with you."

CHAPTER 7

The path Blanche took ran by the river for a few yards then branched off among the trees and shrubs. It twisted and turned through thick foliage for almost half a mile before it came out again by the river. Half afraid of facing Sam, Blanche slowed her pace. What would she say to him? What if he wouldn't listen? What if he wouldn't come home with her? What if he wasn't there? Blanche almost turned back, stopping for just a moment to decide. It was then that she got the feeling she wasn't alone, a feeling that she was being followed. Had she heard something? a crunch on the gravel path behind her? a rustle of leaves? or was it her imagination playing tricks after her mother's warning? She listened for a moment. Hearing nothing she walked on. As her feet crunched on the path she heard the sound again - almost an echo of her own footsteps. Yes, there it was again, she was sure of it, crunch, crunch, just a second after the sound of her own feet. Again she stopped to listen. Again the noise ceased. She looked back over her shoulder. She could see nothing through the trees but she knew someone was there. Now she hurried on but so did the sound of the feet that followed. Faster, faster, step for step with hers. Calm down, she told herself, don't be daft, it was probably Sam or Paul trying to frighten her but she wasn't convinced. Her heart started to pound, thump, thump, thump, in time with her feet.

"Please, God," she prayed, "I know I've been wicked to Sam and I'm sorry. Mam told me I'd be punished for what I've done but please, I don't want to be murdered. Please help me."

Above the beat of her heart she heard the crunch of feet getting nearer. If she could get to the river bank where the trees thinned out, maybe there'd be someone there. Men fishing perhaps. She started to run now and so did the thump of feet that followed. Gasping, she ran ever faster but so did her pursuer. He was close now. She could hear him breathing hard. Then she felt his hand on her shoulder. She twisted away but he grabbed her hair, pulling her backwards against him. Blanche screamed as loud as she could, "Sam! Sam!" Her assailant put his hand across her mouth. It tasted of tobacco. She bit his finger, hard.

"You little bitch," he growled and for a moment his grip loosened as he slapped her face.

She screamed again

Then suddenly Sam was there. "Leave her alone. Get off her." he yelled, jumping on the man's back trying to get a strangle hold round his throat. Blanche was suddenly freed as her attacker tried to release Sam's fingers from around his neck,. "Run, Blanche, run."

But Blanche was on her knees gasping for breath, her whole body shaking. She was sick.

Determined as he was Sam was no match for his adversary. He was thrown off, staggering backwards against a tree. Sam waited there, his back against the trunk, for the onslaught he knew was to come and realised that if he was to hold his own he would have to fight dirty.

When the attack came Sam steadied himself and kicked

out with his foot. The man let out a scream of pain, holding on to his crutch but it didn't stop him for long. Sam found himself on his back from a blow that sent his senses spinning. This is it, he thought, first he'll kill me, then it'll be Blanche. He wanted to shout again for her to run but his breath had left him. A second later he felt the first kick from the man's boot. Desperately he tried to roll away out of reach. Another kick caught him in the ribs. Things began to get a bit muddled after that. His head felt twice its normal size and his breath rasped in his throat. He thought he heard Blanche scream - not a scream of fear this time, or pain, but a scream of sheer fury. Through a misty haze he saw her launch herself at the man, lashing at his head and face with what looked like a bunch of leaves. Sam could only think he was hallucinating.

The kicking stopped with a yell of pain, "You vicious little cow," he heard, and then he heard something else through the buzzing in his head, or was he imagining it - the sound of running feet. He wasn't imagining it. Their attacker heard it too and turning, he quickly disappeared, crashing through the thick scrub at the side of the path.

Sam lay where the man had thrown him, stunned and winded.

"Sam! Sam!" Blanche knelt down beside him, holding his face between her hands. " Oh, Sam! Don't die. Please don't die. I'm sorry, Sam. Real sorry."

That was the scene that met Paul as he came round the bend in the path.

"What's going on? Damn you, our Blanche, leave him alone you bad little bugger. What have you done?" he yelled when he saw the blood on Sam's cheek where

Blanche's hands held him.

Sobbing now, Blanche wailed, "Sam saved my life and nearly got himself killed doing it."

It took some time for Paul to take in what she had said, "Saved your life? I thought you were trying to murder him. What happened?"

"A great brute of a man attacked me when I was looking for Sam. I thought he was going to kill me but Sam came and fought him off. Oh, Paul, he was so brave. Don't let him die, Paul, please don't let him die. He really did save me from being murdered."

"Saved you from being…? What for? If I'd been Sam I'd have let him get on with it after what you did to him."

Sam tried to sit up now and shook his head to dispel the cloud that befuddled him. He'd never been so pleased to see anyone as he was to see Paul. "Don't be daft," he said through thickening lips. "It's my thing, rescuing maidens in distress."

"You've been watching too many Robin Hood films."

"No, he hasn't. Robin Hood would've hidden behind a tree and shot arrows at him - that's not brave."

"Makes more sense"

"No it doesn't."

Paul realised then that Sam was hurt badly. "Oh, do shut up and let's get Sam home. You," he said pointedly to his sister, "can walk behind. I don't want to be seen with you looking like that."

"Beast."

Paul put his arm around Sam and helped him to his feet. "Can you manage to walk?"

Sam nodded, but each step he took was agony.

...

The front door of the Watson's house slammed shut, feet scuffled about in the hall, then Paul appeared pushing Sam and Blanche before him. "Here he is - what's left of him," he announced.

Blanche flung herself into her mother's arms, "Mam! Mam! I thought I was going to die. I thought I'd never see you again."

Hilda hugged her daughter to her, "Oh, love! Whatever's happened? You're hurt. Look at your poor hands, and your face, it's all bruised."

"What the hell's been going on?" Dave glared at Sam but Paul broke in.

"You'd better hear what they have to say before you start jumping to conclusions."

"What happened, Sam?" Roger gently drew his son down onto a chair. He could see the boy was in shock.

His voice barely above a whisper, Sam said, "I was sitting under this tree I go to when I want to be on my own, when I heard somebody screaming, 'Sam! Sam!' I knew it was Blanche so I…" he held his hand to his head to dispel the cloud that was gathering again.

Impatiently Blanche took up the story. "This horrible man grabbed hold of my hair and when I screamed he hit me - and I bit him - and screamed for Sam - and then Sam came and dragged him off me - and Sam said for me to run but I couldn't - and then I was sick." Blanche gasped for breath but before anyone could interrupt she went on, "I fell down on some prickly leaves and they made my knee bleed," she lifted up her leg to prove her story, "look, and when I got up Sam was lying on the ground and he, the man, was kicking him, so I hit him in the face with the prickly leaves and he swore at me and then he ran away." she held out her hands, "Look, those prickles made my hands bleed too."

"That's when I arrived," Paul broke in on the tale, "When I found 'em Sam was flat on his back with Blanche bending over him," he gave a sly grin, "I thought she was trying to murder him."

"You're a brave lad, Sam," Dave put a hand on his nephew's shoulder. Sam winced.

"We should get these two to the hospital pretty quickly and then let the police know what happened. This chap isn't going to get away with this." Roger was in control now, "I can get you all in my car if Blanche can sit on your knee, Hilda."

"Yes, of course," Hilda nodded. "I'll just tidy them up a bit first."

"No!" Roger almost shouted his order. "Leave them. Let the police see what a state they were in when they came back."

"He's right, Hilda," Dave nodded his agreement. "Better let the nurses see to them."

The journey to the hospital was the longest and most painful Sam had ever made. Every bump in the road, every corner they turned, was agony.

...

"Dear me! What have you two been up to to get in a state like this?" was the greeting they got from the nurse.

Sam looked dumbly back at her while Blanche, usually so talkative, said nothing. Roger explained what had happened, with Dave and Hilda adding a word now and then.

"We've called the police," Roger informed the nurse, "Don't you think they should see the children as they are - see the state they came home in?"

The nurse shook her head, "The police will have to wait."

It was at that moment the police arrived in the form of Sergeant Gill and a constable.

"Don't I know you, young man?" he grinned at Sam. "You're the one who got himself boarded up in a council house." Sam was in no mood to appreciate the Sergeant's banter. He just wanted to lie down and die, "Now," the sergeant took out his notebook when he realised his joke wasn't going down too well.

But the nurse intervened, "Not now, if you please. These children are in no fit state to answer your questions, they're in shock and this boy's in a lot of pain so the sooner we get him attended to and into bed the sooner we can make him comfortable." and she hustled the sergeant and his constable out of the room.

"But, but…" the Sergeant started to protest. He wasn't used to being ordered about but the nurse was adept at dealing with awkward customers. "No 'buts'," she said firmly, "You can see them tomorrow if they're well enough."

"It looks as though he's cracked a rib and possibly fractured his elbow. We'll be able to see better when we've X-rayed him. There's bad bruising to his face but no permanent damage." the doctor told Roger after his initial examination.

"So he'll be staying in here tonight, I take it?"

"Maybe longer. We'll have to assess his injuries tomorrow."

"...and the girl?"

"Just bruising. She's in shock, naturally. We've told her parents she must be kept in overnight but she'll be well enough to go home in the morning."

Roger said, "I'll be in to see Sam tomorrow. Here's my 'phone number in case I'm needed," and he handed the doctor his card.

Roger kept his promise and the following evening found him sitting by Sam's bed looking down at his sleeping son. Pride welled up in his chest at the thought of Sam's bravery. Not many lads of his age would have stood up to a grown man especially in defence of someone who hated him as much as that girl seemed to. The nurse interrupted his thoughts.

"He's had a bad night," she said, hovering around Sam's bed straightening the cover, smoothing his pillow, "but he'll be fine in a few days. It's just rest he needs now."

Sam opened his eyes.

"Hello, son, how are you feeling?"

"Dad!" Sam's voice was barely above a whisper but Roger heard.

'Dad' he'd called him. If ever there had been any doubt in Roger's mind that Sam was his son, that word and the emotions it aroused in him dispelled any such doubt. Gently he pushed back the boy's fair hair from his forehead.

"You're going to be OK, son."

"I thought I was going to die yesterday," Sam said through the corner of his swollen mouth.

"Don't talk if it hurts. I can do the talking for both of us." Roger paused and smiled down at his son. "The nurse tells me I mustn't stay long in any case. But what I wanted to say was that with the summer holidays coming soon I'd like us to take time to get to know one another better, if that's OK by you. We will go anywhere you fancy. We'll have a great time together; make up for all the years we've lost. What d'you say?" Sam nodded eagerly and tried to smile. "But in the meantime I want to know what to do with you when you come out of here. Will you go back to Dave's?"

"Dunno."

"It'll be alright with them. Hilda wants you back. Even the horror wants you back. You're a hero now."

If Sam could have shrugged his shoulders as he usually did at times like this, that would have been his only comment. Instead he just blinked.

"Well, we'll leave it for now. Just think about it, eh? It's your best option though, Sam."

"I think he should rest now," the nurse bustled in once more and pummelled Sam's pillow again.

"See you soon then, son."

"See you."

...

Hilda held her daughter close in the back seat of the taxi that took them home that morning and looked at her anxiously. "Sure you feel alright, love?" The ordeal of the previous day had taken a lot of the bounce out of Blanche. She scarcely said a word as they left the hospital.

"Yes, Mam." Blanche lowered her head fractionally. It still hurt. "Is Sam going to come home soon? He said he wouldn't before."

"I hope he will, love. I don't know for certain, though."

"I *think* I said I was sorry but I can't be sure. It's all so mixed up."

"It must be, love, but I'm sure he'll know you're sorry now, even if you didn't say so."

Blanche nodded and closed her eyes until, ten minutes later, they arrived home.

"I think you should go and lie down for a while, at least until your Dad comes home."

Blanche was only too pleased to go to bed. She felt shaky and very tired. All she wanted to do was sleep.

It was teatime before Blanche came downstairs.

Dave greeted his daughter with, "How are you feeling, love? I came upstairs to see you but you were fast asleep."

"I'm OK, I think," Blanche was still bleary eyed from sleep. "I don't want any tea, Mam."

"Perhaps you'll feel like something later on, love, eh?"

Blanche nodded absentmindedly, her thoughts were on Sam.

"Mam, can we get Sam something nice when he comes out of hospital?"

"Yes, of course, Blanche. We'll think of something. He'll need some new clothes for a start. They had to cut his others off while he was in hospital."

Blanche showed her impatience. "No, not clothes. How about a bike?"

Hilda marvelled at her daughter's change of heart.

"Well, I suppose we might manage a bike, we'll see."

"He did it for me, Mam, even after what I'd done to him, so I'd like us to get him a bike. I know he wants one."

"He's a good lad, is Sam." Dave fondly stroked his daughter's hair, "Yes, I'm sure we can manage a bike for him."

Dave had barely finished his meal when the doorbell rang.. Hilda hastily cleared away the dirty dishes while Dave opened the door. It was Sergeant Gill.

"I called to see how the children were." the Sergeant stood holding his hat in his hand in the hope of being invited in.

Dave recognised the significance of the Sergeant's bare head and opened the door wide. "Blanche is home," he said as he led the way into the front room where Blanche sat with her mother, "but Sam's still in hospital."

"Still in hospital, is he, and how are you, young lady?"

Blanche muttered something about being OK.

"Bad business, this." the policeman said as he sat down at Dave's invitation. "I've been to the spot. You can see where the attack took place, there's still signs of a scuffle and we found a holly branch with blood on it. The one used in the fracas, no doubt. If we can eliminate this young lady's blood group, any other blood we find on there must be the attacker's."

Hilda sat stoney faced while the Sergeant spoke. When he paused she said, "I think it's shameful that our children can't walk in the park without being molested. We could have lost them both. What if he'd had a knife? Something's got to be done."

"We've put a patrol on that path. It's a real danger spot

I agree and we've got the Council to cut down some of the shrubs to open it up. That way there'll be nowhere for these bu…..beggars to lurk. Now, what I came about," he leaned forward to get his notebook from his pocket, "was to see if Blanche here feels well enough to give me a bit more information."

"I'm alright." Blanche told him without much enthusiasm.

"Well, then, can you tell me anything about this chap? What did he look like? Was he dark or fair? How tall was he?"

Blanche nodded to confirm that she understood. "I remember that he put his chin on the top of my head when he first grabbed me. That was before I bit him."

"So, let's see, how tall are you, four foot ten to five foot? That would make him about, say, five foot eight or ten. Did he have dark hair or light?"

"It was dark - greasy and he had a bald bit right on top. I saw that when he was kicking Sam."

The Sergeant wrote all this in his notebook, "What about his face? Did he have a beard or a moustache?"

"No but he needed a shave and he smelled of cigarettes."

"His clothes now. Can you remember what he was wearing?"

Blanche had to think about this. "They were dark," she screwed up her eyes the better to remember what she had seen. "He had a jumper on. It felt rough and smelled sweaty. I *think* it was dark blue."

"Anything else you can think of, Blanche?"

Blanche shook her head.

"Any birthmarks, scars, tattoos?"

"YES." she shouted the word in the excitement of remembering, "I saw it when he was bending over Sam. It was up his arm. It looked like a fish's tail curled round. I couldn't see the rest of it, it was covered with his sleeve."

"Could it have been a mermaid's tail, d'you think?"

Blanche nodded excitedly, "Yes, yes, I think it could."

Sergeant Gill grinned broadly and to Dave he said. "We've got the blighter. If it's who I think it is, we've been after him for years. But he's a slippery character. Oh, yes! It's him alright. Thank you little lady. Thank you very much. There's just one more thing I must ask you. Would you come and identify him when we've brought him in?"

Blanche hesitated. For a moment fear showed on her face, but she nodded. "I suppose so."

"Brave lass. But don't worry. He won't see you, We'll make sure of that."

...

Sam sat up in bed, a sling on his left arm. The swelling on his face had gone down considerably, making it easier for him to talk as well as being less painful, which was a blessing because Sam had plenty of news for Roger when he next visited him.

"Mr Fenwick came to see me this afternoon," Sam told his father proudly, "and he brought Mark with him."

"Who's Mr Fenwick, and who's Mark?"

"He's my teacher and Mark his my best friend - after Paul, that is." Sam paused for a moment while he wriggled into a more comfortable position.

"Very thoughtful of Mr Fenwick…and Mark."

"They came to tell me that I will be going to Grammar School in September, and so will Mark."

"Good for you, son. That's great news."

"I'm glad Mark's going because I wouldn't have gone on my own."

"Why not? Why wouldn't you have gone without Mark? Look, Sam. if you wait for other people to do things with you all your life, you'll never get anywhere."

"Well, I won't know anybody there."

"So?"

"I always feel daft going anywhere on my own."

"You'll get over that. I have to go places where I don't know anyone, places where they don't even speak English. It's a case of gritting your teeth and getting on with the job, see? Like you did with that chap the other day. You didn't feel daft about tackling him, did you?"

"Guess you're right, Dad. I hadn't thought of it like that."

"You've done well, Sam but don't let 'feeling daft' as you call it, spoil your life. I'm proud of you, and you mother will be proud of you too, won't she?"

"Mam'll be wondering where I am. I told her I wasn't going to stay with Uncle Dave anymore. She might not remember but sometimes she does."

"Want me to go and see her for you?"

"Would you? Would you, really?"

"If you want me to."

"If you do go will you say I'll come and see her as soon as I can and tell her I love her?"

"I'll tell her. I'll go while I'm nearby."

Roger kept his promise to Sam and that same evening found him in the waiting room of the hospital asking for Amy.

"Amy Watson?" the woman asked, "Come with me, she's in here." and she took Roger into the patients' lounge where Amy sat dozing in a big chair by the window.

"Miss Watson." the woman shook Amy's shoulder gently, "You have a visitor, dear."

Only half awake, Amy asked, "Is it Sammy?"

"No, love. It isn't your son."

Roger said, "Hello, Amy. How are you?" He tried hard to hide the shock at seeing her this way. The once beautiful girl with the long blond hair now looked like a witch. Her face was drawn and grey, her cheeks deeply lined and her eyes, those eyes that had held so much love and happiness, were dull and sunken. Had he done this to her? What a selfish brute he'd been. "It's Roger," he said in answer to the question in her eyes.

"Roger?"

Had he too changed so drastically that she couldn't recognise him?

"How are you, Amy?" he asked again and took a chair opposite to where she sat.

Amy nodded and gave him a thin smile, "Where's my Sammy?"

"Sammy's alright, Amy. He asked me to tell you that he'll be coming to see you as soon as he can."

"But where is he?" Amy persisted.

Roger put a comforting hand over hers, "Now you're not to worry. He's in hospital but he's alright."

"In hospital? This hospital? He's hurt, my Sammy's

hurt?"

"Now, now, don't get upset. He's going to be alright. I told you. He's a brave lad, our Sammy." and he told Amy the saga of the attack on Blanche and how Sam had gone to her rescue. " I'm so proud of him, Amy."

"But he's hurt."

Roger patted her hand. "He asked me to tell you not to worry and he sends you his love."

"He's a good boy, my Sammy."

Roger nodded his agreement.

...

It was another three days before Sam went back to Dave's, his arm still in a sling. Everybody made a fuss of him, telling him how brave he was, and much to his embarrassment his Aunty Hilda would keep putting her arms around him and kissing him, saying, "I'll always be grateful for what you did for Blanche."

Sam's one ambition was to get away, to make a beeline for his willow tree but escape was impossible, even Roger seemed intent on barring his getaway. Only Blanche, after her first kiss, stood aloof, smiling, a smile Sam knew of old meant that she was up to something. It made him nervous, and positively scared when she eventually took hold of his hand and said, "I've got something to show you, Sam. Come on." and she led him out of the back door and into the shed followed by all the rest of the family. "Here you are, Sam. This is for you." and she wheeled the bike towards him.

No one had ever given Sam such a present as this but it wasn't the cost of the present that awed him it was the fact that this was something just for him. His to keep. Words just wouldn't come. He held the handlebars with his good hand, walked it around, spun the peddles, tried the brakes and then managed a "Gosh! Thanks."

"Well, aren't you going to try it," Paul asked.

"How can he with that sling on," Blanche said disparagingly.

"Gosh! It's smashing but I'll have to wait till I can take this thing off my arm."

"Won't be long, son." Roger comforted him.

"Come now," Hilda ordered, "Dinner's ready. Go and wash your hands, the lot of you."

Roger stood for a moment waiting for Sam. "Sorry I couldn't collect you from the hospital. I got held up at a Council Meeting."

"It's OK, Dad. I'm glad you've come, though. This homecoming lark's a bit overdone, don't you think?"

"I can see what you mean," Roger whispered later on when Blanch sat on the arm of Sam's chair,

"He's my hero," she announced, twisting a lock of his hair around her finger.

"Get off," Sam laughed, pulling away from her, but Blanche was unabashed.

"I'm going to marry him when I'm old enough."

Paul winced, "Hasn't he suffered enough, poor bugger?"

"That's enough of that," Dave feigned anger but couldn't restrain a smile. Paul had echoed his own sentiments.

By this time Sam was desperate to get away from all this attention, so when Roger announced his departure Sam offered to see him to his car.

"Cor! Dad this is awful. Take me with you."

Roger shook his head. "Bear up, Sam. It won't last."

"I can't stay here, Dad. Did you hear what Blanche said? She's going to marry me."

Roger threw back his head and laughed "Don't worry about that, son. Just don't commit yourself. OK?" and still laughing he drove away.

Sam watched the car till it turned the corner, 'Don't commit yourself,' his father had said. How d'you manage that with a girl like Blanche?

PART II

CHAPTER 8

"Are you two ready yet?" Dave called from the bottom of the stairs where he waited impatiently with Sam and Paul, all three of them done up in their best and ready for the party.

"Coming, love. I'm just doing my hair."

"That'll be another half hour at least. Blanche!" he yelled, "Get a move on."

"Won't be a tick," Blanche's voice came muffled. She was applying her lipstick, a tricky operation when you're expected to speak as well.

Dave lifted his head and tutted, "Women! Those two have been up there for the past hour. What are they doing? If there was any improvement I wouldn't mind but... WHAT THE ...?"

Blanche tottered half way down the stairs in her new high heels and spread her arms, "De dah!" she heralded. "How do I look.?"

"Good grief!" Paul gasped.

"Wow!" came from Sam.

"Bloody hell!" Dave's face went puce. "You can take all that muck of your face right now, young woman."

"Aw, Dad.!"

Hilda, from the top step asked, "What's going on?"

Blanche turned to her mother for support, "Mam?"

"Well! well!" Hilda tried to keep her face straight at the sight of her daughter sporting more make-up on her face than Hilda used in a month. "Come here. Let's have a look at you. That's not bad." she looked closely at her daughter's efforts, "Not bad at all." she frowned and shook her head at Dave to make him hold his tongue, "I think, though," she said, drawing her daughter to the hall mirror, "if we just tone down that lipstick a bit," and she wiped a tissue over the girl's mouth, "dab your eye shadow, like this, to take away the harsh lines, and get rid of the rouge. You have enough natural colour of your own, dear. Now, a dab of powder - dust it off. There, isn't that better?"

Blanche studied her reflection in the mirror with approval. "Yeah. That's great."

"What d'you think, Dave? Doesn't your daughter look lovely?"

Dave had to admit it was a big improvement and said so.

Paul grinned, "She'll do."

Sam said, "She's beautiful," seeing Blanche as a woman for the first time.

Blanche gave him a coquettish smile. "Thank you, kind sir. For that you can dance with me at this 'do.' "

The 'do' was Paul's twenty-first birthday party which Hilda, much against Paul's wishes, had decided was going to be a day to remember. She, together with as many friends and relations as she could muster, had baked and buttered all morning. Now the feast was spread out on the long trestle table in the Committee Room at the local cricket club. The table groaned under the weight of pork pies, sausage rolls, vol au vent, sandwiches of beef, ham, pork, and anything else Hilda could manage to lay hands on. Then there were cakes, tarts, jam sponges, cream cakes, trifles and, the piece de resistance - Paul's birthday cake, made and iced with loving care by Hilda herself.

She led her family now through the reception area and flung open the Committee Room door with a flourish.

"Gosh!"

"Wow!" and

"By gum, that's a fair old spread," came from her family.

Dave asked, "Where's the booze, love?"

"Booze? We're having no drunken orgy here, my lad."

Her husband took a jaundiced view of this. He had been looking forward to a 'few pints' as had Joe Duckworth, Eunice's father. "We've got to toast the lad's health, Hilda."

"I've got some champagne for that. That's all that's needed."

"Won't do, love. I'll go and get a crate or two from the bar." and he went, leaving Hilda to watch him go in disgust.

Paul, when he realised this celebration was inevitable, had hinted at a surprise on the night. Everyone guessed it would be the announcement of his engagement to Eunice.

"It'll save another embarrassing 'do'," he had told her. "If it's OK with you, love, we'll get it over with in one go at my birthday party."

Eunice didn't mind so long as they got engaged because, as she told Paul, it wouldn't be fair on their parents to have the trouble and expense of another party so soon after his twenty-first. It was this thoughtful attitude that Paul so loved in her. For Paul there had never been anyone but Eunice and it had always been understood that when he came of age they would announce their engagement followed soon after by the wedding. Why they supposed it would be a surprise to everyone was hard to say. Eunice's face, pink with excitement that was matched only by Paul's nervousness, told everyone what to expect. And so, when the cake had been cut and Paul's health was drunk, he held out his hand to Eunice and drew her to his side.

"I want to thank everybody for coming this evening and making my birthday such a happy one…."

"He doesn't mean that," Blanche whispered to Sam, "He hated the thought of this party."

"…for the lovely presents I've received and I want to thank Mam and Dad for all that they've done for me, not just tonight but during the past twenty-one years. Now, though it might seem greedy after all that, I'm going to ask Eunice for a very special birthday present." he fumbled in his pocket for the ring, "Eunice, love, will you marry me?" he said, slipping the ring on her finger and kissing her.

"Yes, Paul," she whispered. "Yes, darling, I'll marry you."

There was a roar of applause from the guests and Hilda smiled across the room at Dave, the unspoken pride in her son there for all to see.

The evening went well under Hilda's critical eye. Certainly no one got drunk, although by the time the evening drew to a close the men, and some of the women too, had had their fair share. Even Sam had drunk more than was usual for him.. The band had also 'had a few' and while the rhythm remained steady, a few sour notes crept in here and there as the night wore on. Blanche claimed dance after dance with Sam, not that, at this stage, he had any objections. Blanche snuggled closer then she put her cheek close to his and, as the last dance ended, she kissed him long and hard. He kissed her in return with more enthusiasm than Hilda thought seemly. Her smile, as she watched them, gradually faded, This, she decided, was not on. Oh no! She wasn't having this and she took hold of Blanche's arm and dragged her away.

"I need you to help carry some of this food home," she nodded towards the table and the remains of the buffet.

Sam, slightly befuddled, grinned sheepishly and thought - she's all right is Blanche.

"That was a disgusting display," Hilda told her daughter when she got her alone.

"What did I do?"

"You know what I'm talking about, my girl. I'm talking about the way you kissed Sam in there. What will folk think? He's your cousin, and what's more he's living under the same roof."

"Don't be such a prude, Mam. This is the 1960s, not the Dark Ages. I've told you before, I'm going to marry Sam."

"You are not, madam."

"Oh! but I am."

"He's your first cousin. You can't. Besides…"

"You can marry your cousin. I know. I've checked, and there's no 'besides'."

"Yes Blanche, there is. Think how your children could turn out."

Blanche stared at her mother in disgust. "You mean because of Aunty Amy? She's autistic. It's not hereditary. It's not catching."

"There's more than that to what ails Amy. Don't you think your Dad and me haven't gone into this autistic business?"

"So what more is there?"

"Blanche, be told, you are not going to marry Sam and that's it."

"Really? What if I told him what you've just said?"

"That's up to you if you want to hurt him but I don't think you will."

"Won't I? Well maybe not. Not yet anyway seeing he hasn't asked me but if - when he does.."

"Don't threaten me, Blanche. If he does decide he wants to marry you I shall tell him. Now stay away from him, d'you hear?"

Sam knew nothing of this conversation but he felt the frost in the air and saw the looks Hilda gave him whenever he went near Blanche. He realised he'd overstepped the mark at Paul's twenty-first, for he knew Hilda had a dread of the neighbourhood gossips. She most likely thought they were speculating right now about what happened after the 'do'. Also, knowing Hilda's vivid imagination she probably had visions of him raping Blanche at every opportunity. The thought made Sam smile. It was more likely to be the other way round, knowing Blanche.

...

Sam loved Blanche. He knew it was much too soon to tell her so, even though she'd made it obvious she fancied him. But she was barely seventeen and Sam could well imagine that this was Blanche's idea of a joke. He had suffered her teasing too often to rely on anything she did or said being serious. That didn't alter the way he felt about her though and he decided the best thing he could do for everybody concerned would be to move out. This would put Hilda's mind at rest for one thing and once away from there he could meet Blanche without the gossips speculating as to what was going on behind closed doors at the Watsons. Time would tell whether she loved him or not. So Sam made his mind up to go and live with his father, providing Roger would have him, of course. His father, he knew, valued his privacy. Roger, liked to entertain - mainly his lady friends - so he might consider Sam's presence an intrusion. Anyway, he could ask, and if the answer was 'no' then he'd have to think of something else. Also, Sam needed a reason to move out. After all that Dave and Hilda had done for him over the years it seemed churlish to announce baldly that he was leaving and he could hardly tell them the reason; not yet anyway.

The excuse he needed came sooner than he expected. Dave, Paul and Sam usually went to the football match on a Saturday afternoon but on this particular Saturday Paul cried off.

"I'm meeting Eunice," he told them. "Why don't you go with them Blanche?"

"Yeah! Great!" she said, much to Dave's annoyance.

Hilda watched the three of them go down the garden path and when the gate had closed behind them she turned to Paul, "What is it, love? Something wrong?"

Paul's unease was all too obvious and it was a while before he plucked up the courage to say,

"It's Eunice, Mam, she's pregnant."

Hilda looked closely at her son. This news didn't surprise her. She asked, "How far on is she?"

"We've only just found out; eight weeks, the doctor says." Paul took a deep breath, "Mam, we wondered like… well… there's no room at their house for us, so…" he looked away, his face aflame with embarrassment. Paul had always prided himself on being independent. He hated to have to rely on others, even his own family, but this was a situation he hadn't foreseen and he was desperate. If he'd expected a lecture from his mother it didn't come and this calm acceptance made his feel even worse.

"You're saying you want to come and live here, then?" Paul nodded. "Well," she went on thoughtfully, "your room isn't big enough. We could just about get a double bed in there but where would you put the cot?" Paul sat with his hands deep in his pockets to stop their nervous twitching, saying nothing. He could think of no answer, no solution to this problem.

"I suppose we could clear the front room and let you have that, though what we would do with the furniture I don't know."

His mother's air of weary resignation brought, "No, Mam, you can't do that," from Paul.

"Tell me what else we can do? You'll never find a place to rent these days and buying a house is out of the question. Your Dad hasn't got that sort of money and I don't suppose Joe has either."

Paul shook his head despairingly. "Anyway, Paul," she said more brightly, "we've got a month or two yet. Something might turn up so don't worry, we won't see you fast for somewhere to have the baby. We can't have our grandchild in need of somewhere to lay his head, can we?"

The thought of their first grandchild being born here in this house brought a warm glow to Hilda's heart, a glow that put all thoughts of losing her precious three-piece suite from her mind.

...

"Congratulations, Paul, or do we call you Daddy?" Sam said, slapping his cousin playfully on the back when he heard the news.

Paul pulled a wry face, "It's no joke, Sam. It's happened too soon. We have nowhere to live. There's no room at Eunice's place. Mam's offered to let us have the front room but we feel bad about her and Dad having to get rid of their furniture to put us up. You know how proud she is of that three-piece suite. She would never let us play in there when we were kids, would she?"

"No," Sam laughed, "but it was always the front room that I found myself in when I got a telling off. Seriously though, Paul , there's no problem as far as you and Eunice are concerned. I'll move out. I can go and live with Dad, then you can have my room for the baby. How's that sound?"

Paul's worried look changed to a broad grin, "You'd do that for me?"

"Well, not exactly. I've been thinking about going to Westwood Rise for a while now, only I didn't quite know how to broach the subject with your Mam and Dad. I didn't want to seem ungrateful for all they've done for me since Mam went into that place by moving out just when I've started to earn a bit of money but since I'm working for Dad now, it seems logical to live there. It's so much nearer the works."

Paul put an arm across Sam's shoulders, "You're a pal. I'll tell Mam. No, we'll both tell her but before we do I want to ask you if you'll be best man at our wedding?"

"I thought you'd never ask. Of course I will, old pal."

The relief on Hilda's face when they explained what had been proposed was, Sam knew, not entirely due to the fact that she would now be able to accommodate Paul and Eunice without having to get rid of her precious furniture but to the fact that Sam would be away from Blanche.

"Well, if that's what you want," Hilda smiled at Sam for the first time in weeks, "and Roger's agreeable, is he?"

Sam assured her that he was and so a week later he was all packed and ready to move out, much to Blanche's dismay.

"What d'you want to do that for?"

"I have my reasons," Sam told her.

"What reasons?"

"You'll find out."

CHAPTER 9

With a phut, phut, phut, a loud bang and a cloud of smoke the Morris Minor came to a shuddering halt at the kerb outside Dave's house where Sam and Paul waited. The off-side door opened, Mark unfolded his lanky body from the car and joined the other two on the pavement.

"What d'you think of her, then?"

Paul walked slowly round the little car, "Bit of rust along the bottom of this near side door. You want to get that seen to before it falls off. Back bumper's loose too." he winked at Sam, "Needs a bit doing to it, Mark. How much did they rush you for it?"

"Fifty quid." Mark was beginning to look uneasy.

"You were robbed."

"Rubbish! There's nowt wrong with her that I can't fix. The engine runs real sweet. Flossie'll be like new when I've seen to a few things and given her a lick of paint."

"FLOSSIE!" Sam raised his eyebrows, "You call it FLOSSIE?"

"Yeah!" Mark grinned, "after my Gran, 'cos it's little and farts a lot."

Hysteria took over. Sam and Paul fell into each other's arms to support themselves.

"You can laugh but you haven't got a car, either of you, and if you want me to take your things over to your Dad's, Sam, you'd better apologise."

Still shaking with laughter Sam said, "I'm sorry, Mark,

but calling it FLOSSIE! Does your Gran know?"

"D'you think I'm mad? She'd skelp me for sure. Come on, get your belongings in the boot. Time's money, you know." he said in the most business-like manner he could muster.

Mark had bought the old Morris Minor cheap but even so it had left him broke. In an attempt to recoup some of the cost he was hiring it out for small jobs like the one he had now - taking Sam's things to The Garth.

"Where did you say you wanted to be?" he asked as he released the brake and pressed his foot on the accelerator. The car jerked forward a foot or two then stopped. Mark swore and tried again with more success this time. "You'll have to put your arm out of the window when we turn left. The indicators don't work."

Sam did as he was bid.

"Where are we going?" Mark asked again.

"Westwood Rise. It's the other side of town, off the Harrogate Road."

"I know it. Bit posh round there."

"It's where Dad lives."

Mark gave Sam a sidelong look, trying to fathom whether his friend was pleased to be leaving his Uncle Dave's or not. He had always had the impression that Sam was never happy there, though nothing had ever been said. "You going for good?" he probed.

"Yes." Sam didn't elaborate any more than that and they fell silent while Mark manoeuvred Flossie through the town.

Sam's feelings, as they made their way to his new home, were mixed. He knew that Hilda was glad to see him go and wondered now whether Roger really wanted him living at the Garth. His father, he had to admit, had not hesitated when Sam asked if he could move in but there was that niggling doubt in Sam's mind that just would not go away. Would it work out? Would they get on all right? What did his father expect of him? These doubts kept Sam silent for most of the journey and Mark's voice saying, "We're here. Which house is it?" brought him back with a start.

"Here?" he asked, "That was quick."

"I don't muck about, you know. Which house?"

"The Garth. That's it over there to your right."

"Blimey!" Mark exclaimed, "Your Dad lives there?"

Sam shrugged. He felt embarrassed by Mark's admiration. "It's just a house."

"I'll give you a hand if you like," Mark said, struggling out of the driving seat.

"It's OK Mark. I'll dump my stuff inside the gate and collect it later."

"Right." Mark felt a pang of disappointment that he wouldn't get a look inside this house where Sam was going to live. He had often wondered what these places looked like from the other side of the door because it was his ambition to own one some day. "Right." Mark said again. "I'll be off then." but still he made no move to get back into the car until Sam remembered he had made a deal with him.

"Sorry, Mark, I nearly forgot to pay you." and handed over the agreed amount.

Mark grinned, waved a salute, and saying, "See you, mate." drove off with a screech of tyres.

Sam stood for a while in the driveway, his bits and

pieces strewn on the ground around him. He had always been a little in awe of this house and now it was to be his home. Standing in its own gardens, its tall trees shielding it from the world outside, its wide front door and wide windows looking to Sam's eyes most imposing, the Garth dwarfed the house he and his mother had shared. He had been here many times since he had first met his father and his visits had made him familiar with the ground floor rooms; the hall with its mosaic tiled floor and wide staircase; the front room - lounge, Roger called it - with its white marble fireplace, dark red leather chairs, red velvet curtains at the windows that reached from ceiling to floor and the Indian carpet that seemed to swallow your feet in its deep pile; the dining room across the hall with its long table and carved dining chairs - Chippendale, Roger said they were - its huge windows draped with the same deep red velvet as the lounge and the mahogany side table that stood against the wall holding serving dishes that Sam imagined could contain enough food to feed the whole street. Behind the third door was Roger's study, a room book-lined and dominated by his desk and the captain's chair that was upholstered in green leather, like the top of the desk. The only other door in the hall lead to the kitchen, a huge room that housed a big square deal table and walls that were lined with cupboards. Pans hung from a rack over the AGA while by the back door a fridge, that must have been one of the earliest on the market, rattled and shook incessantly. The only other door in this room opened into a walk-in pantry whose shelves held dozens of pots of home-made jam and pickles. Sam wondered whose handiwork this was - certainly not Roger's. Outside the back door, what had once been the kitchen garden, was now a scrubby lawn kept under control by Brown, the man Roger employed as a casual gardener. All this was familiar to Sam but the upper floors would be new territory to him.

"So, you've come home at last. Welcome, Sam." Roger's voice broke in on Sam's thoughts and the warmth of that greeting allayed the doubts he had had about being wanted. "Where's the rest of your stuff?" When Sam nodded to the three cases and two cardboard boxes by the gate, Roger's "Is that all?" echoed Hilda's remarks ten years earlier. "Come on then," Roger took hold of the cases, "let's get these inside and I'll show you your bedroom."

Sam. with the rest of his belongings, followed his father up the wide curved staircase and onto the upstairs landing. Throwing open a door at the top of the stairs Roger asked, "Will this do?"

Dropping his luggage Sam looked around the room that was to be his, "Great. It's great, Dad."

Roger nodded, "I'll leave you to put your things away then we'll eat, shall we?"

For a while, after his father had closed the door behind him, Sam stood by the window looking out on the lawn and the flower beds, the orchard and beyond to the paddock. So much space, Sam thought, so much peace and quiet, so unlike the hubbub of the Council estate. No kids here yelling and fighting, no radios blaring from every door, no women screeching threats at their offspring. It seemed like heaven to Sam and he spent quite a while just trying to take it all in. As he turned from the window he caught a glimpse of himself in the triple mirror that stood on the dressing table and grimaced. He must get a haircut. New life, new image, he decided, sitting on the edge of the bed. He bounced up and down a few times. Oh, yes! This was luxury. In this bed he could stretch his limbs and turn over without fear of falling out as he had a few times when he first went to live at his Uncle Dave's. Yes, he liked it here, liked it very much. But he smiled when he looked inside the wardrobe and realised that the few clothes he had would be lost in that cavernous piece of furniture.

"You coming, Sam?" came from downstairs. "Your meal's ready."

"Coming," and Sam hurtled down the stairs and into the kitchen where Roger stood dishing out the food,

"It's only bacon and eggs. I don't profess to be a brilliant cook. Mrs Meredith will fix us a meal tonight."

"This is fine, Dad. I like bacon and eggs." Sam didn't add that he'd already eaten bacon and eggs for his breakfast.

That evening Sam and his father sat under the trees in the garden enjoying the evening sun and drinking wine from delicate glasses, a new experience for Sam. Roger, in a sombre mood said,

"You don't know how pleased I am to have you here, Sam. Everybody needs a family; someone to love and care for."

Sam, looking down into his glass, said, "I'm pleased to be here too. I never felt wanted by Hilda. She'd be OK one day and off me the next. I didn't know where I stood with her."

Roger nodded understandingly and for a while they sat in friendly silence.

"Can I tell you something, son?" Roger said eventually, "I've been wanting to explain about your mother and me. Not that I'm trying to vindicate myself, I just want you to hear my side of the story." Roger traced the rim of his glass with his finger. "My marriage to Stella was a disaster. I can't blame my father for that but I did feel that I was pushed into marrying her because her family and mine had been friends for years. Maybe push isn't the word. Eased into it is a better way of putting it perhaps. We rowed incessantly from the start, Stella and I. I wanted a family. I've always been fond of children, but the thought of being pregnant and having kids under her feet appalled her." he shrugged his shoulders expressively, "I took refuge in my work at first and then, well I knew it was wrong but I looked for love elsewhere. It wasn't just one women either I'm afraid, until I met your mother, that is. Oh, Sam! she was so beautiful. Those snaps you have don't do her justice. You should have seen her. Blond hair that waved softly to her shoulders, expressive eyes - one minute laughing, the next sad. She had such a beautiful face and she was so sweet natured too. I fell hopelessly in love with her. I couldn't help myself. She had other boyfriends, I knew that but I was determined to win her for myself. That year with Amy was the happiest time of my life. How anyone could think she had a mental problem I can't imagine. She was naïve, yes; childish in a way, but then she was only seventeen. When she told me she was pregnant I was really happy. I planned to divorce Stella and marry Amy. Then I made the mistake of telling my father. He and I had a dreadful row. I walked out and that was another mistake. If only I'd stayed to find out what he was up to I could have put a stop to it. You see, what I found out later, much too late in fact, was that he went to see your Gran and, knowing they were hard up, he offered her money, more money that anyone in her circumstances could refuse. Amy was sent away until after you were born. My father, it seems, insisted that you be given up for adoption but he reckoned without your mother. She refused to let you go. When I went to see you and your mother your Gran wouldn't let me into the house. She told me Amy didn't want to see me and that you weren't my son anyway. I realise now that she was too afraid of what my father would do. You see, he had promised to support you and Amy after he realised his attempt to get you adopted had failed, so long as they denied you were my child." Roger said angrily, " Amy must have thought I was a callous brute not to have visited her but it wasn't until after my father died that I found out he'd been paying a monthly cheque into Amy's account and I realised then you must be mine. After that I kept up the payments. Sam, I want you to know that I never had any intention of hurting you or Amy."

Sam bowed his head, "I'm glad you told me this, Dad. I honestly never heard Mam say a mean word about you and I suppose I took my cue from her. She'd tell me how handsome you were," he laughed self consciously, "and that I took after you, and what a kind considerate person you were. The only thing I resented was being called a bastard all my life but it was the folk who used that word about me that I hated, not you. I have to say that I was mad at you when I found out you were loaded and we had gone hungry after Gran died. When I got to know you though, I realised you wouldn't have let that happen, not knowingly."

Roger smiled, a tight smile that didn't dispel the sadness in his eyes, "All the heartache your mother must have suffered doesn't bear thinking about. I'm so sorry, Sam, so very sorry."

Sam's nod of agreement was all that was needed to affirm the understanding between father and son.

CHAPTER 10

The day Paul and Eunice were to be married dawned bright and clear. A beautiful Spring morning.

"Happy the bride the sun shines on," Hilda told her son as they waited, all spruced up, for the wedding cars. "I hope that goes for the bridegroom too, Paul."

"I'll be happy with Eunice, Mam, you can be certain of that." Hilda held her son in an emotional embrace, "Mam, don't cry. This is my wedding, not my funeral, and we are coming back here after."

"I'm alright, Paul," she patted his shoulder and gave him a watery smile, "It's my right to be a bit weepy at my son's wedding."

"Oh, Mam!" and Paul hugged her to him.

"Paul, the car's here," Blanche, still in her dressing gown, yelled from the hall.

"Aren't you ready yet? Don't you mess things up for me today, Blanche, or I'll never forgive you."

"I *am* ready. I'm not going to put my frock on yet. I don't want it all creased up, do I?" she reached up and uncharacteristically kissed his cheek. "Be happy, Paul."

For some reason that Paul couldn't explain, this simple gesture from Blanche brought a lump to his throat. He could only kiss her cheek, then he was gone.

Hilda watched as he walked down the path, out through the gate and into the waiting car. Tears blurred her eyes. Her son. Her kind, gentle son would soon be married. It didn't seem possible that so much time had passed since he was a fair-haired little boy with wonder in his blue eyes. Soon he would belong to another woman; soon he would be a father. "Oh, Paul!" she whispered, "Darling, Paul."

Dave too felt emotional about this wedding. He and Paul had always been close, as close as any father and son could be. He reflected that Paul had never been any trouble even in his school days. No, there'd never been a bit of bother with Paul. There had always been a maturity about him that often amazed his father. He had reason, he told himself now, to thank God for this son of his. Now he was a grown man, soon to be a married man with all the responsibility that that entailed. Soon too, he'd be a father, with all the trials and tribulations plus the love, that children brought. Silently Dave prayed that his son would be happy.

In the little church close by where Eunice lived with her parents, Sam stood beside Paul. The vicar had already schooled them in their roles for the ceremony but even so Paul was visibly nervous. He asked, "Are there many here, Sam?"

"Well, have a look. You've only to turn your head."

"Not likely. You tell me."

Sam turned and did a quick estimate of the congregation. "About forty or fifty, I should think."

"Where did all that lot come from? I thought it would only be close relatives."

"Shows how popular you are." Sam grinned. "Come on, Paul, relax. You're not going to be hung, drawn and quartered. You're getting married to Eunice - you remember Eunice, do you?"

At last Paul smiled. Yes, Eunice. His lovely Eunice. He bet she'd be feeling nervous too.

It was at this point that the organ struck up the wedding march and all the congregation stood and turned to watch Eunice, holding tight to her father's arm, walk up the aisle followed by her two bridesmaids. The congregation gasped at the sight of the little group. Eunice, in a dress of pale peach that set off her auburn hair and hazel eyes; her attendants, in dresses a shade deeper than the bride's, Janet, her sister, dark-haired, doe-eyed with a timidity about her that was so very appealing, and Blanche, with her pale hair, blue eyes and delicate features that so belied her determined character.

"Aren't they all so beautiful," someone whispered behind Sam and Paul. The two looked at each other and smiled. Blanche caught Sam's eye and lowered one eyelid. Sam winked back. Paul and Sam joined the little group as they came to the chancel steps, and the ceremony began.

All the right responses were made and no one gave reason why 'these two should not be joined together in holy matrimony'. Paul kissed his bride tenderly, shyly, and then they were led into the vestry where the register was duly signed and the marriage was sealed. All those nearest and dearest to the bride and groom made their way to the Duckworth's where Eunice's mother had laid out a buffet for the guests.

"That went well, didn't it?" Joe Duckworth announced with a much needed glass of whisky in his hand and a look of relief in his eyes. No one had asked if he was nervous. No one said, 'How are you feeling, Joe?' but Joe's legs had all but given out as he escorted his daughter up the aisle.

This event had been even more nerve racking than his own wedding he decided but which, if asked, he would have had to admit he could barely remember now. But it was over and he could relax. Now for the booze.

Wisely, Gladys Duckworth had insisted on the formal speeches being made as soon as they were all back at the house, before the menfolk got at the drink.

"We'll get no sense out of 'em after they get a few pints down their throats," she confided to Hilda.

Hilda agreed.

"Come on, Sam. Do your stuff." someone urged.

So Sam made his prepared speech, which everybody applauded and said was so very appropriate to the occasion. Paul, still nervous, hung on to Eunice's hand while he delivered his short speech - and short it was. After his thanks to everyone concerned, he sat down with a thump and a sigh of relief. He leaned towards his new bride, "I'll be glad when we can get away from this, won't you?" he said in an undertone. Toasts and speeches over, the male guests made for the beer.

"Aye, I've been gagging for this," Joe said as he raised his glass to Dave, "That's one lass's wedding over. Just one more to go. After that we'll be flat broke."

Dave raised his glass in response. "I'm in the same boat, mate. Another ''do' when our Blanche gets wed and then I can relax."

"Is she courting then, your Blanche?"

This, in view of Hilda's opposition to Sam, was an awkward question to answer. Dave said, "Aye well, off and on, your know." which seemed to satisfy Joe's curiosity.

As soon as she could extricate herself from the well-wishers, Eunice quietly crept upstairs to change and then, after much back slapping and teasing, the happy couple set off on their honeymoon in Morecambe, paid for by Sam as a wedding present.

"You're a pal." Paul hugged his cousin, "Thanks, Sam, for everything." he said by way of farewell

CHAPTER 11

Sam, as soon as he left school, had started to work for his father. Roger made it clear from the start that Sam was not going into a 'cushy job'.

"You'll have three months in each workshop until you get an idea of what goes on there. You'll finish up in the Drawing Office. I intend to set up a design centre for a new venture I've had in mind for the past year - making moulds for plastic components - and if you shape up I'll put you in charge.

I know you're capable of it, Sam, so what d'you think?"

"Sounds great, Dad. That's just the sort of thing I want to do. I have a lot of ideas floating about in my head but until I see how things work here I won't be sure whether they're practical or not."

Roger nodded, "I'm going to put George Hollingsworth in charge of you. George is a good chap. He worked for my father and he knows the job inside out, so listen to what he tells you."

It was Sam's turn to nod, "Yes, of course."

"Just one word of advice. Don't get involved with the women here. I did. Not just your mother either, and it makes life very complicated. Keep your social life separate, Sam."

Sam lifted his eyebrows and wondered if his father considered him one of the complications. In any case, as he explained to Roger, he had no intention of seeing anyone but Blanche.

All this Sam related to Blanche the following day but his enthusiasm didn't seem to communicate itself to her.

"Don't you think that's great?"

"Yes, great," she said, flatly.

"You might sound a bit more excited about it."

"Sam," Blanche twisted her fingers together in her lap, "Mam's been going on at me for seeing you."

"Why? Why should she object to us seeing one another? I moved out so she'd feel easier about us. I know how she feels about the neighbours gossiping if it gets around we were," he laughed at the thought of using an old-fashioned word like "courting."

"Well she does object. She says," and Blanche swallowed hard to control her tears, "if we get married and have children she thinks they might be…be.. like your Mam."

"Like Mam? But she's autistic, not mad, and that isn't…"

"I know. I told her that but she thinks there's more to your Mam's condition. She thinks.. well she didn't say exactly what she thinks but it's obvious that both Mam and Dad consider there's something else wrong with Aunty Amy. Something more than autism. Some brain disorder."

"I'll come and talk to her, shall I?"

Before Sam had chance to go and see her, Hilda arrived on the doorstep at The Garth. It was Roger who opened the door to her knock, "Hilda! Come in."

The look on her face told him this was no social call.

"I've come to see Sam."

"Sam? Oh, yes, Sam, " normally Roger would have yelled from the hall to tell his son he had a visitor but he had more than a feeling there was trouble brewing. He felt he had to warn his son that the dragon was after his blood. "I'll go and tell him you're here. He's in his room." Roger didn't ask Hilda to sit down., He wasn't sure what the reaction would be.

"Your Aunty Hilda's here looking fearsome," he told Sam, "I think you should buckle on your sword. It looks like there's going to be a fight."

So Sam squared his shoulders as he faced his Aunt. "Hello Aunty Hilda. I was about to come and see you."

"So you know what I've come about. then?"

Roger raised his eyebrows at Sam. Hilda caught his reaction. "Do you want me to say what I have to say in front of your father?"

"Yes, of course," Sam was pleased to have Roger's backing. When Hilda was in one of her rages it was a comfort to have someone with you who you knew to be on your side.

"Right, then," metaphorically she rolled up her sleeves, "To start with you've been seeing Blanche behind my back."

"No, Aunty Hilda, I've done nothing behind your back. I've taken Blanche out a few times since I left your house but I don't see …."

Hilda cut short his explanation, "Once is too much, my lad."

"I don't understand. Why shouldn't I take Blanche out?"

"It's serious, isn't it, this thing between you and our

Blanche?"

"I suppose it could be. I love her if that's what you're getting at."

"It's got to stop. I'm not having it. You and Blanche are cousins - same family - same blood, it's not right."

"You're talking about my Mam, aren't you? You seem to think her condition runs in the family and I could end up like her but she's autistic, I'm not."

Hilda shook her head slowly from side to side, "It's more than that and you know it. Amy's going mad, anybody can see that."

"I don't know anything of the sort."

"Just a minute." Roger had listened carefully to this interchange and realised it was going nowhere. "You think Sam could end up like Amy?"

"Quite easily."

"In that case," there was a sardonic smile on Roger's face, "surely your husband is even more likely to 'go mad' as you put it. He has exactly the same blood in his veins as Amy. Sam, on the other hand, is my son and carries my genes too."

This came as something of a shock to Hilda. She had never once considered the possibility that Dave could be anyone but Dave, that he could become like his sister and it made her even more angry.

"You're talking rubbish," her voice rose with her temper.

"You know I'm not, don't you?"

"I know nothing of the sort and I won't stay and listen to such rot. But I'll tell you this, Sam Watson. I won't have this carry-on between you and our Blanche. If I have to I'll get a Court Order out to stop you seeing her, she's under age." and with that she opened the door and slammed it behind her.

Sam was stricken. "She can't do that, can she?"

"I'm afraid she can, Sam."

"What do I do, Dad? I never intended to upset Dave or Hilda like this but I love Blanche."

"The easiest way would be to do as she says and wait until Blanche is twenty-one. That way there's nothing Hilda can do about it."

"Four years!"

"Four years isn't that long if you really love one another."

...

"I've been to see Sam." Hilda told her daughter when she got home, "and he tells me he doesn't want to see you again."

"I don't believe you," Blanche's eyes blazed. Her mother was lying. She must be.

"He doesn't want you to have brain-damaged children any more than I do. He says I've to tell you to keep away from him."

"NO, Mam, he wouldn't say that, not Sam. I'm going to see him."

"You'll only get hurt if you do. He told me it was all a lark anyway, that he'd never had any intention of marrying you or anybody else for that matter, not for a long time yet. He's in with his father's posh friends now. We're not good enough." silently Hilda asked forgiveness for all these lies but she would have done anything to save her daughter from getting involved with anyone who could hurt her. If Sam went mad he might be violent, he might beat her, even murder her, who knows. She couldn't let that happen, not to Blanche.

When she thought about what Roger had said it frightened Hilda. She looked at Dave now in a different light. But no, there was nobody more sane than her Dave. A bit daft at times, perhaps but never mad. Although, she had to admit, he had a heck of a temper when he was roused. Yes, she'd have to watch him.

After the visit from Hilda, Sam was desperate to let Blanche know that he loved her, that he'd wait four years - forty if need be. He knew better than to go to Dave's so he waited outside the office where she worked but there was no Blanche. When, in desperation he asked one of her colleagues where she was he was told she hadn't been at work for the past week. He sought Paul's help, but Paul had troubles of his own and told him so. "What d'you want to bother with our Blanche for after the nasty tricks she's played on you? No, mate, I'll not get involved. You're better off without her."

When Sam eventually did see Blanche it was obvious she was trying to avoid him.

"Blanche," he pleaded, "I must talk to you."

"Go away," she snapped. But Sam persisted and caught hold of her arm.

"LET GO OF ME" and she slapped him a stinging blow across the face that stopped him in mid stride.

Holding a hand to his cheek he stood and watched her walk away from him. He hurt, but not from the blow so much as from the venom in her voice.

"Blanche!" he called, in one last attempt to make contact with her, but she ignored him.

CHAPTER 12

Sam was angry. Angry with himself. For the first time since his mother had gone into ‘that place’ as he called the Mental Home, he didn’t want to visit her. It wasn’t that he didn’t want see his mother, it was the thought of meeting up with Hilda after that stormy scene at The Garth that brought this reaction. Sam had no intention of starting up the argument about his seeing Blanche again, not in front of his mother. He had always tried to shield her from anything unpleasant, from anything he thought might upset her, though he knew she sensed when he was unhappy. She would pat his hand and say ‘Don’t worry, Sammy love’ and give him that sad smile of hers that always made him feel like hugging her and telling her how much he loved her.

Today, Sunday, Hilda and Dave would be paying their weekly call at the Home and he would have to join them for the two hours they were allowed to visit. He debated with himself whether he should stay away or not. At least if he did Hilda wouldn’t have cause to voice her opinions and his mother would be spared the indignity of hearing that they thought she was insane. But his mother needed him. He had to go for her sake. Finally, Sam decided that if Hilda took up the argument again, he would make an excuse and leave.

It was a surprise, a pleasant surprise, to find his mother alone that Sunday afternoon. No doubt Dave had kept Hilda away to save his sister any unpleasantness. Sam gave a silent thank you to his uncle. The afternoon passed pleasantly for Sam and his mother. She seemed happy, never once questioning why her brother and his wife hadn't come. They talked of the times they lived at number twelve. Sometimes Sam had to remind her of the things that had happened, about things his Gran had said and done, about the time he'd come home covered in mud after falling in the stream that ran the other side of the railway line.

"D'you remember how mad she was at me?" Sam asked. His mother smiled sadly and he knew she didn't. "She sent me off to bed without my tea. I was starving."

"Poor Sammy," Amy gently touched his cheek.

"I suppose I deserved it. We used to play dangerous games too like daring one another to cross the line when the train was coming. How we got away with it I'll never know."

Amy shook her head and giggled, "You were a naughty boy sometimes, Sammy."

We could never have talked about things like that if Hilda and Dave had been there, Sammy thought as he made his way home that afternoon. With them the conversation consisted of "How are you, Amy love?" "Are you feeling any better, Amy love?" "Do you like it here now, Amy love?" What a boring pair they were. But Sam's conscience pricked. He knew he shouldn't think that way, not after they'd looked after him all those years. He supposed he was put out by the fact that they wouldn't let him see Blanche, and then again, Blanche's rejection of him made him bitter too. Yes, that had hurt him more than he liked to admit even to himself and it was six months before that hurt began to heal; six months of trying to persuade himself that there was no point in moping after Blanche if she didn't love him, though he found that hard to believe; and it was six months after that meeting with Blanche when she'd slapped his face, that he met Sandra.

Sandra, the very opposite of Blanche, was tall and dark with an elegance that matched any of Roger's lady friends. Both young women, it must be said, were beautiful in their own way but for Sam Blanche was the love of his life and he had no intention of getting too involved with Sandra. He enjoyed her company very much and was proud to be seen with her. That, for Sam, was as far as it went and mistakenly he thought Sandra felt the same, so when it was suggested he should meet her parents it came as somewhat of a surprise, for Sam realised the implications of this invitation. No immediate excuse came to mind and Sam found himself committed to calling on Mr and Mrs Robinson the following weekend.

Roger raised a quizzical eyebrow when Sam told him.

"I know. I know," Sam said angrily, "You don't have to say it. I always seem to get myself into this sort of mess, even without trying."

"Do what I always do, Sam."

"Yes, you told me once before. '*Don't commit yourself.*' It didn't work then, either."

"Only because you didn't really want it to."

So Sam, with knees quaking, found himself on Sandra's doorstep that Sunday evening. The tall, rangy woman with thin lips and jutting chin who opened the door, almost dragged him inside.

"You must be Sam," she said, "Come in. Come in," and she grabbed his arm, announcing as she pushed him into the sitting room, a room cluttered with objects d'art on every conceivable surface, and furnished with an overstuffed three-piece suite in green moquette, piled high with cushions, "Here's Sam, father. Sandra, come and introduce us properly, dear."

Sandra put a possessive arm through his "Mummy, Daddy, this is Sam Watson. Sam, my parents." and she brushed an imaginary speck of dust from his shoulder.

Mr Robinson rose to the occasion, "Pleased to meet you, my boy." and shook Sam's hand like a pump handle.

"My! You do look smart, Sam." Sandra simpered, much to Sam's embarrassment.

"Thank you," was all he could think of to say and wished he hadn't come.

Embarrassment followed embarrassment.

"Don't they make a lovely couple, father?"

"Indeed they do, mother."

"Now," Mrs Robinson beamed at the two men, "you two get to know each other while Sandra and I prepare the supper." She gave her husband a knowing look and pushed Sandra towards the kitchen. At that moment Herbert Robinson looked more embarrassed than Sam. He cleared his throat.

"Yes, er well…sit down, lad. Make yourself comfortable. They'll be back with the supper shortly. Well now, Sam," he sat in the armchair near the fire and leaned towards his visitor. "Our Sandra's fair taken with you, son. She's a good lass, is Sandra, but you know that, of course."

Sam recognised the signs. He was being vetted. Was he son-in-law material they wanted to know?

He heard the echo of his father's warning, 'Don't

commit yourself, son.'

He smiled at the older man, which Herbert took for agreement. "And what do you do for a living, Sam?"

Careful now, Sam told himself. "I work for Wilmott's Engineering."

"Wilmott's eh? I know Roger Wilmott quite well. Yes, quite well. Nice chap, Roger. He's done well for himself since his father died."

Tongue in cheek Sam asked, "Perhaps you could put in a good word for me then, sir."

"By all means, lad. By all means. What, may I ask, do you do at Wilmott's?

"I'm in the Drawing Office."

"Draughtsman, eh? Does he pay well, Wilmott?"

"Fairly well, I suppose, but you know, Mr Robinson, I have plans for my own business, like you.

I admire you, sir. Sandra has told me how you built up your own business. Nobody to tell you what to do. Everything you earn is yours. That's what I call enterprise."

Herbert Robinson flushed with pride. "Well, though I say it myself, as shouldn't, what I've achieved I've done without help from anybody. Never borrowed a penny in my life. Never."

Sam breathed a sigh of relief. He'd parried the questions, at least for the time being. Now he guessed he would have to sit and listen to Herbert's life story. Better that though, than the inquisition they'd planned for him.

"Yes," Herbert Robinson gazed into space and slowly nodded his head. "I've worked hard to get where I am today and it's been hard work, Sam, I'll not pretend it hasn't."

"I realise it must have been." Sam said encouragingly.

"I started with ten pounds. Just ten pounds, Sam. I bought a box or two of apples and oranges, a few vegetables and set out my stall in the front room of my parents' house. Ten pounds, that all I had but I never looked back." he made an expressive gesture with his hand. "All this, everything you see here, is mine. All paid for - house and all. I don't owe a penny."

"That's amazing."

The older man nodded, "Not a penny."

Mrs Robinson appeared with a tray of cups and saucers followed close behind by Sandra carrying sandwiches and cakes. Eleanor Robinson caught the last few words spoken by her husband.

"Has he been boring you with his life story, Sam?"

"Oh, Daddy! You haven't."

"Yes, well er.." Herbert began.

"It really was interesting," Sam felt obliged to defend his host. "You must be proud of what Mr Robinson has achieved."

"Proud!" Eleanor exploded.

Sandra nudged her mother, "Yes, we are very proud of you, aren't we Daddy?" she sat on the arm of his chair and kissed the top of his head.

"That's right," his wife recovered her temper, "indeed we are."

Supper was a delicate affair. Delicate china, delicate little sandwiches, delicate little fairy cakes, nothing like the hefty meals Hilda prepared. Sam ate half-a-dozen sandwiches without feeling he'd had anything before he noticed his hostess's raised eyebrows.

"Delicious," he said.

Placated, Mrs Robinson smiled. Sam went home hungry.

"What a charming young man," Sandra's mother remarked after Sam left. "Such nice manners, my dear."

Sandra smiled, "I told you so, didn't I?"

After her husband's failure to extract the necessary information from Sam about his prospects and his background, Eleanor Robinson made plans to vet Sam herself, a task that took her the best part of a week. What she discovered shocked her. What shocked her still further was her husband's reaction when she told him her news.

"Well, does it matter?" he asked. Herbert had taken a liking to this young man who listened to him so attentively. He had never had anyone applaud his efforts before but he knew, even before he said it, that his feeble attempt to champion Sam, was doomed to defeat.

"DOES IT MATTER!" she shrieked, "DOES IT MATTER!"

"Will you tell her?" Herbert growled.

"We'll both tell her. You have to back me, Herbert."

The front door slammed shut.

"She's here. Now remember." Eleanor's tone was threatening.

"Hi, Daddy. Mummy."

"Sandra. We have to talk."

"Talk? Talk about what?"

"Your young man."

"Sam?"

"Yes Sandra. Sam isn't all he appears to be, my dear. I feel…we feel… your father and I, that you shouldn't see this young man again."

"Not see him? Why, for goodness' sake? You were so impressed when you met him."

"That was before. I've been hearing things," she said mysteriously, "and they are not very nice I can assure you."

"Things? What things?"

"His background, darling, is not at all suitable. Your father has his own business, Sandra. We have standards to keep up."

"What are you talking about?"

"Sam Watson is illegitimate," Eleanor announced with great deliberation as if such a thing was a criminal offence, "and what is more, his mother is in an asylum."

Sandra bit her lip. She'd rather set her heart on marrying Sam. "That's hardly his fault, is it?"

"Perhaps not, dear, but he's not the sort of young man we want you to associate with."

"But, Mummy…"

"Now don't argue, Sandra. Your father agrees with me," she looked to her husband for confirmation but Herbert averted his eyes. "We know what's best for you. Just think what might happen if you married. Why, your children could be mentally retarded. Do you want children who aren't right in the head? Well, do you?"

"Of course not, Mummy, but…"

"Well, then?"

Sandra was a level-headed young woman who never did anything without considering all the pros and cons of a situation. "I'll have to think about it," she announced sharply and before her mother could raise any more objections she got up from her chair and went to her room. Once there she sat on the bed staring disconsolately out of the window and thought about Sam. Though she'd known him only a short time Sandra had decided that this was the man for her. Sam had been so different from any of the other men she'd dated. Sam was attentive and thoughtful. He had confidence without being brash or overbearing, added to which he was very good looking. All her friends were envious of the fact that she was dating him. Then, as a bonus, he didn't seem to be short of money.

These were the pros; as to the cons, Sandra knew that life would be intolerable if she ignored her parents' advice, not that, should she decide to marry Sam, she couldn't put up with her mother's nagging. But Sandra recognised the logic of their argument. Could she, she wondered, endure a lifetime of looking after a child who was mentally subnormal? Sandra knew her limitations, knew her patience soon wore thin, and what if..? Her brain reeled at the thought that if Sam should… No. She could never put up with that - never. Her decision was made.

...

Sam watched as Sandra walked slowly towards him on their next date. He should have realised something was wrong, that the eagerness had gone out of her step, that there was no enthusiasm in her greeting. This was not a meeting she looked forward to. Usually Sandra had no qualms about breaking off a relationship but with Sam it was different. For one thing she felt ashamed of the reason for her actions, for another, she was loathe to tell Sam these reasons. It would seem, she realised, as if she had been prying into his affairs, as indeed her mother had. Why, oh why couldn't the woman keep her nose out of other people's business, out of her daughter's business in particular?

Sam greeted her with "I've booked a table for eight o'clock so we've time for a drink beforehand if you like." he kissed her. She didn't respond.

"Sam," Sandra hesitated, "Sam, I can't come with you tonight. I'm sorry."

"Why?" Sam looked closely at her. She looked as though she had been crying. "Why not?" he asked again.

Sandra shook her head, "I'm really sorry but I shan't be seeing you any more."

"You've found someone else?"

"No, Sam."

"Then why?"

"I just can't. Don't ask me why."

"Surely you owe me some sort of explanation," his tone of voice gave her no other choice but to tell him the truth.

This was the moment she had dreaded. Sandra took a deep breath. Words came pouring out. Words her mother had said and she added, "because of your mother being where she is and the fact that she's not married."

It was a tactless way to put it. She'd had a speech prepared but it had come out all wrong. She hadn't wanted to hurt him but the look on his face told her that she had, and badly. Inwardly she cursed her own stupidity. At least they could have remained friends if she'd been more tactful but she realised that was impossible now.

Sam looked at her as though she had struck him. Visions of Hilda and her tirade against him came to mind.

"I see," he said through clenched teeth.

"I know it isn't your fault, Sam," Sandra tried to placate him, "but Mummy says if we…" Suddenly Sandra realised she'd made things worse. Sam had never mentioned marriage, nevertheless he got the message. He understood perfectly. Here it was again. His illegitimacy and the fact that his mother was in a mental home was being thrown up at him.

He was livid. "If that's how you feel then it's OK by me. I hope you find somebody worthy of you," he added sarcastically. Turning, he walked away, leaving her standing alone on the pavement. Faster and faster he walked until in the end he was running. Where? He had no idea. Why? Yes, he knew why. He wanted to get away from his birthright, get away from the slurs, the insults that had been thrown at him all his life, running, running until he found himself in the park. He stopped to catch his breath and realised then that running away was pointless. He wasn't a child anymore, sitting under the willow, wallowing in his misery. He was a grown man. He had to face facts and the facts were obvious. He had to live with these things no matter what the consequences were. He remembered Roger's advice when he was young,. 'Grit your teeth and get on with life, Sam.'

Slowly he made his way back to The Garth and his father.

"I thought you had a date tonight," Roger realised as soon as the words were out of his mouth that something was very wrong.

Sam reverted to his boyhood trait of shrugging his shoulders. "She doesn't want any more to do with a bastard."

"Did she say *that*?"

"Not in so many words. Her father, she tells me, has a position to uphold because of his business."

Roger spluttered. "His what? He's a greengrocer for heaven's sake. Do they know your my son?

Sorry. That sounds pompous, but really!"

Sam felt himself relax. "No, they don't, and if you're talking pompous, they don't come any more pompous than that family" he laughed now at the memory of his meeting with the Robinsons. "Now that I've told you, now that I've said my piece out loud I feel better. I've had a lucky escape, don't you think?"

"You weren't serious, were you?"

"No, but she was," Sam's grinned.

"You booked a table at Toni's didn't you?"

Sam agreed that he had.

"Then why don't we go a celebrate your lucky escape?"

CHAPTER 13

A month or more elapsed after Hilda's visit to The Garth before she and Dave came to see Amy again. An uneasy meeting for Sam when Hilda's greeting was a mere nod in recognition. Dave said, "How are you, Sam?" in an apologetic tone but offered no explanation for their absence, greeting Amy in their usual way, "How are you, Amy, love?"

Sam looked on, feeling the tension between them. The conversation during the first half hour was general and Sam was beginning to relax when Hilda, with a sly look in his direction said,

"We've got some exciting news for you Amy. Our Blanche is engaged to be married."

Sam froze. So that was why they'd come - to watch him squirm.

"Aren't you happy for her?" she looked peeked that Amy had said nothing.

"Very nice," was Amy's only comment.

"She's engaged to Mark Lowe," turning to Sam, she smiled sweetly, "Friend of yours, isn't he?"

"Yes, he is," Sam smiled stiffly back. "I must congratulate him next time I see him."

"You must come to their engagement party next Saturday," Hilda was revelling in this situation but Sam's reply was quick and to the point.

"Can't make it next Saturday I'm afraid. What a shame.

I have a heavy date."

"Bring your young lady with you," Dave suggested, taking it for granted it was a female Sam was meeting.

"It's nice of you to invite us but I'm afraid everything's arranged."

Sam wasn't exactly telling lies. His date was indeed heavy. He was helping George to rearrange the Tool Shop, and nothing, he thought, could be much heavier than those machines in there. Right now, though, he was determined not to let his misery show but when he caught his mother looking at him with such love and pity it was nearly his undoing. At that moment he wanted to feel her arms around him as he had when he was a child, wanted the comfort she always gave him when things went wrong, wanted her to tell him, 'It'll be alright, Sammy love.'

That night Sam dreamt he and Blanche were married. There was a cottage, the sort of cottage dreams are made of with Virginia creeper up the wall and roses round the door. Two small children played on the lawn while he sat with his arm around Blanche on the garden wall. It was when the two young boys came running towards them that the dream became a nightmare.

"NO! NO! Oh, Lord! NO." Sam woke screaming.

In the next bedroom Roger woke with a start. For a moment he couldn't place the sound, then he realised it came from his son's room. Quickly he pulled on his dressing gown.

"Sam? What's wrong? What's all the noise about?"

Sam was sitting up in bed holding his head in his hands. Without looking up he said, "I'm OK, Dad. I…I. was having an awful dream."

Roger sat on the edge of the bed. "Come on, Sam, get it off your chest. Tell me about it."

Hesitantly his son began to tell his nightmare. "…and then the children turned to us. Oh God! they both had my Mam's face - pale and drawn and old looking." Sam dropped his head onto his chest.

"Come on, Sam," Roger gently stroked his son's hair, "let's go downstairs and have a drink. It'll steady your nerves and help you to sleep."

"Do I want to sleep when I have dreams like that?" nevertheless he followed his father into the lounge.

Roger poured them both a drink and watched as Sam let the whisky trickle slowly down his throat. It burned into his stomach, warming him, relaxing the knot that twisted inside him. His father saw the colour coming back into Sam's face, saw his hunched shoulders relax and asked, "That better?"

Sam nodded.

"It's time we did something about these problems of yours, Sam."

"Yes, but what?"

"Either you confront Hilda about the lies she's obviously told Blanche or you have to put it all behind you and forget her - find someone else. If you take my advice you'll do the latter."

Sam didn't fancy either of these options, "Hilda? You know how formidable she can be. Not that I'm afraid to have it out with her, but I doubt I'll get very far, and she's obviously convinced Blanche that there's no future for us. As to finding someone else, it's all very well but when they know my background, like Sandra, they'll turn against me. It's been like that all my life - 'Your Mam's mad.' 'You're a bastard.' Who would want to marry me? I don't think I can take any more."

"Stop it!" Roger was angry at Sam's attitude. "Blanche and Sandra are only two. There are plenty of women who don't have that cruel streak. I know you must blame me for your troubles and perhaps you're right but I am trying to make amends. I care very much about you, Sam. You must know that and I've been thinking. What d'you say about changing your name to Wilmott? That would tell the world that we're father and son. I'd like that."

Sam looked away, "I am who I am, Dad. I wouldn't want any girl I married thinking I'd deceived her by not telling her the whole truth."

"I don't see it that way at all. Anyway, it's an idea. Think about it." Roger paused and considered the situation further. "There's another thing you could do."

"What's that?" Sam's voice was emotionless.

"Hilda, when she came here and made all that fuss, said she and Dave thought Amy was suffering from something more than just autism."

"Yes, I remember but what can I do about that?"

"Let's get a specialist to see her. That way you'll find out whether what Hilda says is right or not. If, what your mother suffers from isn't hereditary, then she'll have no reason to stop you seeing Blanche. On the other hand, if it is, then you're no worse off than before."

"But the hospital doctor says…"

"The hospital doctor hasn't a clue. He has thirty or more patients to look after. He isn't going to spend all his time on one. Besides, he's not a specialist, is he?" Roger got up and put his glass on the table, "Now go back to bed," he could see Sam's eyes were heavy with sleep, "and we'll talk about it tomorrow."

Sam nodded. He was exhausted. The whisky had done its work and made him drowsy. He was glad to do as his father suggested.

...

Anthony Dowling-Smythe was the name of the specialist Roger came up with. Tony Smith, as he was known to Roger, was an old school friend. Though they hadn't been close, they had kept up a spasmodic correspondence over the years - Christmas cards and a short letter now and then.

A few 'phone calls to Harley Street, where Dowling-Smythe had his clinic, resulted in a very amicable meeting, together with an expensive meal, paid for by Roger, after which, full of good food and rather too much wine, his old friend was all too ready to arrange a consultation with Amy, especially as he knew Roger could afford the exorbitant fees he asked. What is more, Roger discovered that Dowling-Smythe still had a clinic in Manchester which he visited once a month. It was here he began his career and, maybe for sentimental reasons but mainly because he had a very lucrative practise in the North, he was loathe to dispense with it. This Roger realised, would be very convenient for Sam and his mother so he arranged the appointment there for the following month. Roger told his son, "You can take your mother in my car, it's more comfortable than yours," In fact Roger reasoned that the Rolls would impress Tony Smith more than Sam's old VW

Beetle, "and you have to take her medication with you," he added. "Tony needs to know what drugs she's on."

"Right, Dad. Thanks. But do you think the Matron will make a fuss about giving me this medicine?" Sam had vivid memories of his encounter with the woman when he was younger.

"I don't see why but I'll sort her out if you come up against anything you can't handle."

"I'll manage."

Sam faced the Matron on the day prior to his mother's appointment with Dowling-Smythe. He had disliked this woman ever since Dave's confrontation with her nine years before and over the years their mutual hatred of one another had grown. Now, she was being downright unreasonable. He knew he had a fight on his hands.

"I can't just hand over a patient on your say-so." the woman snapped.

"But I've already explained. I'm taking my Mam to see a specialist."

"I've only your word for that, Mr Watson. I cannot let Miss Watson leave this hospital without some sort of authority."

"Oh! for goodness' sake what d'you think I'm going to do to her?"

"The point is, that she is in my charge and I am not prepared to let a patient come and go on the whim of a relative. It isn't as if Miss Watson is capable of making these decisions for herself."

"But she has an appointment with Mr Dowling-Smythe, as I keep telling you. If you don't believe me, 'phone the clinic."

"It isn't my place to do that."

"Then let me do it."

"Certainly not."

"This place," Sam was beside himself with frustration, "is a bloody prison."

"How dare you swear at me, young man."

"I'll tell you how I dare, Miss Jones. It's because you are the most exasperating woman I have ever come across."

Before the Matron could reply, the 'phone rang. Sam, who had been pacing the floor in his agitation, sat down with a despairing thump. Watching the woman across the desk he saw her expression change with the tone of her voice.

"Why, yes, Mr Dowling-Smythe. Yes, of course it's alright. I'll see to that too. Mr Watson is here now. Right I'll tell him. Thank you, Mr Dowling-Smythe. Goodbye." the Matron replaced the 'phone in its cradle. "Mr Dowling-Smythe says he'll see you tomorrow at eleven o'clock. And that, Mr Watson, is the authority I need."

"Well, thank you," Sam said sarcastically, "at last we're getting somewhere."

"I'll see Miss Watson is ready when you come." she said dismissively.

Sam merely inclined his head. "Nine-thirty," was his only comment.

...

The journey, that Friday morning, was a traumatic experience for Amy. She hadn't been in a car since the day they took her away from number twelve. At first she resisted all their attempts to get her into the Rolls but Sam's insistence finally persuaded her to sit beside him in the passenger seat. It was soon evident, as they crossed the town, that this was a mistake. Amy flinched at every vehicle they passed. He could see how frightened she was, so eventually Sam stopped the car and got his mother to sit behind him in the back seat where she couldn't see the oncoming traffic. This seemed to calm her and make her feel safer. Sam talked to her all the way and that too helped her to relax. All the same it was a relief to them both when they drew into the driveway of the clinic. Amy stumbled out of the car, glad to be on firm ground again but bewildered by the strangeness of her surroundings. The double doors of the clinic stood open to the Summer sunshine, welcoming them in. Sam led his mother up the steps and into the reception area where they were greeted by a young woman who showed them into a specious, elegantly furnished waiting room with French windows that looked out onto a well kept garden. It all spoke 'money'.

"I'll just tell Mr Dowling-Smythe that you're here," the young woman told them. "Please, make yourselves comfortable." she smiled and left them.

Sam took his mother to an easy chair by the window where she could look out on the garden. Amy, he knew, loved flowers but today her thoughts were on what was to come and she barely noticed the blooms. She was afraid and told him so.

"Don't worry, Mam. This chap's only going to ask you a few questions. You'll be OK. I won't leave you if you don't want me to."

"No, don't leave me, Sammy love." she pleaded.

Anthony Dowling-Smythe was a sharp-eyed dapper

little man with a bald head. He bounced into the room, shook Sam's hand, asked after Roger, then after making himself known to her, propelled Amy into his Consulting Room where he helped her to a seat. In that touch he felt the tremor of her fear and said gently, "Now don't you worry, my dear, we're just going to have a little chat over a cup of tea. Would you like this young man of yours to stay?"

"Yes." she gave him a frightened look then turned to her son, "Don't leave me, Sammy love."

"I won't, Mam," and Sam put a comforting arm across his mother's shoulders.

For over an hour they talked. Sam marvelled at the way Dowling-Smythe drew the answers he wanted from Amy without her realising it. Amy even managed a smile now and then. Something Sam rarely saw.

Finally he asked what medication she was on..

Amy shook her head, "Just some pills."

Sam handed over the parcel the Matron had given him. Dowling-Smythe took out each packet and examined it carefully, raising his eyebrows at some of the tablets but he made no comment until he replaced them in the bag.

"Mmh! Very interesting." he addressed Amy, "I've received your notes from the hospital, Amy and what I've read intrigues me. I should really like you to spend some time with us here at the clinic. Would you like that?"

Amy gave Sam a worried look. "I want to go home, Sammy."

Sam held her hand while Dowling-Smythe said, "I tell you what I'll do, my dear. I'll take you round the clinic and show you where you will sleep. It's a nice room, I can assure you."

Reluctantly Amy, holding tight to Sam's arm, accompanied the little man to the private rooms along the corridor. Sam had to admit they were very comfortably furnished, each with its own bathroom and toilet, wardrobe and dressing table.

"This room would be yours, Amy." he opened a door on the left of the corridor. "There's a nurse on duty all night so that if you need anything you just have to ring this bell." and he showed them the bell push over the bed, "and you have a nice view of the garden from here, you see."

Amy shook her head.

"Is it essential that she stay?" Sam asked.

"If I'm to make a proper assessment of her condition, then yes, it is. While your mother is autistic to a degree there is definitely more to her problems than that. Whether it is to do with the drugs she's taking I can't say unless I have control of her intake."

Sam nodded his understanding. "Mam, I think you should stay. It won't be for long and as soon as Mr Dowling-Smythe tells me he's finished the tests, I'll come for you."

Amy looked frightened. "Must I, Sammy?"

Dowling-Smythe answered for Sam, "Nobody can force you to stay, Amy but I would like to see if I can make you well. You do want to be well again, don't you?" Amy gave a whispered "yes". "You are a very interesting case, do you realise that?" then turning to Sam, "I feel sure that there's some simple reason for her overall condition and it really intrigues me."

"What d'you say, Mam?"

Amy nodded but without enthusiasm.

"Good girl. Now, I'll ring for the nurse and we'll get your mother settled in, then you can sit with her for a while. In the meantime perhaps we could have a little talk, Sam."

The nurse took Amy reluctantly away, while Sam went back to the Consulting Room with Dowling-Smythe who sat himself behind the desk, drew out a file together with a notebook and took a pen from his pocket. "Now, according to these notes, your mother's age is thirty-eight. Is that correct?" Sam agreed that it was. "From her appearance I should have put her age well over fifty. Incredible."

Sam frowned. Was this man doubting his word? "I have a photograph here," Sam took the snapshot from his wallet. "The date and her age are on the back."

"This is your mother? She was a very beautiful young woman. No wonder…." He was about to say 'no wonder Roger was crazy about her' but he thought better of it and bit his lip. Instead he said, "She looks healthy enough there. You know, Sam, I feel confident we can do something for your mother." he got up from his chair and came round to where Sam sat. "We'll go and see if she's ready for us now, shall we? You can stay with her as long as you wish - up to eight o'clock. That's bedtime for our patients."

Sam held out his hand to the other man. "Thank you. You've given me hope. I really thought…well, that she wouldn't be with us much longer."

"I doubt she will if nothing's done for her but, as I said, I'll do my best and we'll see you in a month's time. Please give my regards to Roger."

"She's staying a month?" Roger's voice rose in mock

horror when Sam told him the news. "That little runt'll salt me for all I've got."

"I've still got some money in my account, Dad. I've saved a bit."

"Don't worry. I'm only joking but he certainly knows how to charge. He always was a money grabbing little bugger when we were at school."

...

"What d'you think you're playing at?" Dave's face was red with rage. "I go to see my sister and they tell me she's not there. Gone to some clinic or other with you. Don't I rate, eh? Couldn't you have told me what you were up to? Don't I get a say in what happens to her anymore?"

This came with Dave's visit to Westfield Rise on the Sunday following Amy's move to the clinic. It seemed to Sam that the only time his family came to see him was when they had something to complain about. Dave ranted on without pause until Sam could stand it no longer.

"Will you let me get a word in, for goodness' sake? I did let you know. I left a message with Eunice the day after I took Mum in. That was on the Saturday, and as for you having a say in what happens to her, you've made no effort to do anything for her in ten years. Something had to be done. She was dying."

Dave's face registered shock, "Dying? Amy? No, lad, your wrong."

"The specialist confirmed it. He says if nothing's done she won't be with us much longer."

"The specialist said that?" Dave's mouth dropped open and he looked down at his feet. "Bloody hell! I knew she was getting worse, but… and you say you told Eunice?

When was that?"

"Saturday "

"Aye well, she must have forgotten. She was taken into the Nursing Home last Saturday. That's why Hilda and I couldn't go and see Amy. What with one thing and another this week's been a bugger, it really has; Eunice going into hospital - she's had a lass by the way - then Amy disappearing, and you know what Hilda's like."

Sam nodded. He certainly did know what Hilda was like, "I'm pleased about the baby. Are they both alright?"

"Aye, they're both fine. Paul's over the moon about it. Anyway, I'm sorry, Sam. I shouldn't have gone on at you like that."

"No you shouldn't. Now are you going to listen to what I have to say about Mam?"

"Go on."

Sam recounted what had happened at the clinic. How Dowling-Smythe had persuaded his mother to stay for a month in order that he could assess her condition and keep track of everything she ate.

"So what happens next?"

"We have to wait until they know the results of these tests."

"It's going to cost a pretty penny, this."

Sam was still angry at the way Dave had confronted him. He said sarcastically, "Don't worry, Roger's paying."

"So he should."

"Now wait a minute. It isn't his fault she's ill."

"That's a matter of opinion," Dave lifted his head and looked at Sam now. "Don't let's quarrel, lad. I've said I'm sorry," he gave Sam a wry smile, "We don't seem to get on very well these days, do we?"

"No, and I'm sorry about that because I know you've done a lot for me but I'm hurt at the way I've been treated over seeing Blanche. It wasn't necessary for Hilda to be quite so brutal in what she said. She came here in a terrible rage, just the way you have today, shouting and screaming at me. She said some awful things until Dad told her that you were more likely to follow in Mam's footsteps than I was, seeing that she was your sister."

Dave looked up sharply, "So that's what's up with her. She's been funny with me for weeks now. Keeps staring at me when she thinks I'm not looking. Queer woman, Hilda. You never know when you have her. Never know how she's going to react. She thought Amy was going off her head and that it was in the family. That's why she fought you so hard. She got the idea you might go mad and beat Blanche up, even murder her."

"She's got a vivid imagination, that woman."

"You're right there, and when it comes to defending her young she's like a tiger. I don't think for a minute that she really meant to hurt you."

"No? Well she did. I'm a grown man now and I won't be treated that way."

"Don't bear a grudge, Sam, let it go now, eh? Let's shake on it and I promise there'll be no more trouble from me. I can't promise the same for Hilda, though." On the step Dave turned and said, "You'll let me know how Amy goes on, won't you?"

"Yes, I'll let you know."

CHAPTER 14

The four weeks Amy was away passed all too slowly for Sam. Twenty-eight days of worrying about how she was, wondering if she was as frightened as when he left her. What were they doing to her? Had they found out what was wrong? When the month was up would she be better or worse? And so it was with mixed feelings that Sam took the call from the clinic that Thursday morning.

"Mr Dowling-Smythe would like you to call at the clinic tomorrow at 10.30 if you can, Mr Watson," the woman at the other end of the 'phone told him.

"Yes. Of course. How is my mother? Is she alright?"

"She's fine, and looking forward to seeing you."

At least, he thought, she was no worse, from what the woman had said. Sam breathed a sigh of relief as he replaced the receiver.

...

Sam's journey to the clinic seemed to take an age. Crossing the Pennines the mist came down, slowing the traffic to a crawl. Wrapped in this blanket of fog Sam felt as though he was drifting through clouds. The only sign that anyone else existed was the red glow of the rear lights on the car in front. His mind wandered back to his childhood with his grandmother and his mother. He remembered how his mother had played with him, danced with him, read to him, taught him his alphabet. Looking back he realised now that his mother had been child-like too. His grandmother would say 'Play with the child, Amy.' and she had played. 'Read to him, Amy' and his mother had read. 'Take Sam for a walk.' and they had walked. Then his Gran had died and Amy had been lost with no one to tell her what to do. Amy had only the basic ideas of how to look after her child or keep the house clean. As for food - cooking was beyond her. His recollection of the meals she prepared made him grimace. If they'd been a wealthy family no one would have noticed that there was anything wrong with this beautiful young f. She would have had everything done or her and being as pretty as Amy was she would have had no trouble finding a rich husband to pander to her every whim. Sam sighed, life was like that, he reflected. When you're rich nothing can touch you, and he determined that one day he would be rich. He'd show 'em. He'd build a house and bring his mother home. He'd pay someone to look after her and she'd live like a princess. That was his dream and he determined to make it a reality.

With a jolt he realised the fog was thinning and soon he was out in bright sunlight but the build-up of traffic into the town delayed him still further. He looked at his watch. He was late. Calm down, he told himself, a few minutes won't make any difference. But he was eager to see his mother, eager to find out if there'd been any change in her condition. At last he pulled into the car park at the clinic, took a deep breath to steady his nerves and rang the bell on the big double doors.

"Mr Watson?" the receptionist asked. Sam nodded. "Mr Dowling-Smythe is ready to see you," and she showed him into the office where the little man sat at his desk.

"Sorry I'm late. It was foggy coming over the moors."

"Don't worry." Dowling-Smythe glanced at his watch, "only fifteen minutes. No problem. Now!" he invariably started business by saying 'now'. Let me tell you what we have discovered. To begin with, your mother is anaemic - a condition which is debilitating in itself - but by far the most important thing we find is that your mother is intollerant to wheat. This is the crux of her trouble. Ah!" he said as the door opened, "here she is."

Sam stood up, ready to help Amy to a seat but she walked in unaided. He couldn't believe what he was seeing. For over a year now his mother hadn't walked without help.

"Mam!"

Amy gave him a smile that said, 'look what I can do'.

"Sammy love," she kissed him and her voice had a new strength to it, added to which there was a set to her shoulders. She no longer stooped. It made her look much younger.

Sam returned her kiss, "Mam, this is wonderful."

"Yes," Dowling-Smyth said, "we're very pleased with you, aren't we, Amy?"

"I'm pleased with myself. I can't believe how much better I feel." Amy told them.

"There's a long way to go yet. We need to put some flesh on her bones," he smiled across at his patient, "and the diet we've devised should help but if you go back to eating wheat products, Amy, it will mean a relapse. We've made out a diet sheet for the hospital. If this," he waved the sheet of paper in front of him. "is adhered to, then hopefully you'll be as fit as the proverbial fiddle in a few months time."

"It's marvellous," Sam shook his head in amazement, "All this time Mam's been," he hesitated. He'd been going to say, 'mental,' instead he changed it to 'sick' which he knew was an inadequate word for his mother's condition but Sam didn't want to hurt her feelings. "just because she's been eating bread."

"Not just bread, young man. There are a lot of foods that contain wheat. You'll see that from the list I've given you. Now, are you ready for home, Amy?" Amy said she was. "First, though, I'd like a word with Sam. Would you go with the nurse to get your things and we'll see you in a few minutes? It won't take long."

Dowling-Smythe waited until the door closed behind Amy and the nurse then, looking at Sam with his head on one side. "Now, what do you think of that, young man?"

"Wonderful, I can't thank you enough, Mr Dowling-Smythe."

"There are two points I would like to stress before you go. I don't want to put a damper on things but this allergy has affected her nervous system over the years. I'm afraid she will never be completely…er.. normal, if you understand me."

"You mean mentally?" Sam suddenly felt deflated.

"Memory-wise for one thing. Perhaps not always grasping the situation she's faced with and then, as I said before, she is, to a certain degree, autistic. There's nothing we can do about that, I'm afraid. Physically, though, as and when we get the anaemia under control, she should be fine. Now take her home and make sure the hospital keep to that diet."

Sam shook the man's hand, "I'll do that, and thank you again,"

Dowling-Smythe laughed, "Thank Roger. He's paying the bill.

...

"You mean all along it's been because she's allergic to wheat?" Sam had been telling Dave the results of the tests Amy had had at the clinic and what the Consultant had said. He had shown his uncle the diet sheet and explained that she must keep strictly to it, otherwise she would be back where she was before.

Dave shook his head slowly, disbelievingly, "It's a miracle. I wouldn't have believed it if I hadn't seen how changed she is."

Sam couldn't help saying, "If she'd had the proper treatment she would never have been so bad."

"Come on, Sam, you can't blame me for that. Doctor after doctor examined her over the years. They all put her condition down to autism."

"Oh! yes, she is still autistic, according to Dowling-Smythe. There's nothing to be done about that, but it wouldn't have made her physically ill. I'm not blaming you, Uncle Dave. I get so angry when I think what she's gone through unnecessarily and how her life has been wasted in that place., Now we've got to watch that the hospital keep to her diet."

"Aye, we have, Sam." Dave paused and shook his head once more, "I must say, this has been a revelation to me. Just fancy, wheat making her like that. I doesn't seem possible, does it? Wait till I tell Hilda. Maybe she'll stop looking at me like I'm daft, now, eh?"

"I doubt it'll change her attitude to me, though."

"Give it time, lad. You never know."

CHAPTER 15

It was a wet, miserable day. Sam had never felt so depressed. For one thing he needed a new shirt and shopping had never appealed to him, not since he had shopped with Hilda for his first suit. Hilda! He didn't want to think about Hilda. Sam had begun to think she had cared about him after that shopping trip. Now he knew different. Women! You never knew how you stood with any of 'em.

He wandered along the High Street looking first in one window, then in another. There was no point in him going into a shop unless he saw what he wanted first. It had to be something smart but not too starchified. His father had suggested he go to a meeting with one of the customers. 'Get the hang of negotiating with clients,' he said. So Sam felt that while he needed to be tidy he didn't want to look like a tailor's dummy. Through the shop window he could see the reflection of passers by. Men like himself, window shopping. Men with their wives, some looking bored, others downright hostile. Thoughtfully he watched them instead of looking at the shirts on display, then suddenly he wished he'd kept his mind on shopping. There, right behind him he saw Blanche and Mark. Sam lowered his head, pretending to be intent on the goods in the window but Mark had seen him.

"Sam!" Mark stood beside him with Blanche holding his arm, "How are you? Sorry you couldn't come to our engagement do. We missed you, didn't we , love?"

Sam realised from this remark that Mark knew nothing of the situation that had existing between Blanche and himself.

"I was pretty busy at the time."

Blanche was looking at him with those blue eyes, troubled eyes. "Sam, how are you…?" her voice ended on a high note as though she would add 'darling'.

Oh! Blanche. Darling Blanche, his heart said but his voice sounded normal, even to his own ears when he said, "OK. How are you? I must congratulate you on your engagement. I hope you'll be happy." And he meant that.

"Thanks, pal," Mark slapped his shoulder. "Never thought I'd be related to you when we were kids."

"Related?" Oh! yes. Cousins," but his eyes were on Blanche.

She looked at him now as if no one else existed. His heart contracted and it took all his self control not to put his arms around her and kiss her. He had to get away. He just couldn't stand being so near her and not being able to touch her. Looking at his watch he said, "I must be on my way. I've a lot of shopping to do."

"Hang on, Sam. Don't go. I just have to get some cigarettes. Won't be a minute," and he hurried into the nearby newsagents.

Neither Sam nor Blanche noticed. They just stood looking into each other's eyes.

"I've missed you," Sam said.

"I've missed you too."

Then as though it was wrenched from him, Sam said, "I love you."

"Sam. Sam, what's happened to us. Why did we let

Mam come between us. She told me some awful lies, I realise that now."

Sam shook his head, "I wouldn't have believed she could do that to us. Anyway, it's too late. You're going to marry Mark."

At that moment Mark joined them again but not before Blanche said, "Am I?"

"How about coming with us for a snack before Blanche and I get down to some serious shopping for the wedding?" Mark pulled a wry face.

"Sorry, Mark. I really have to get back but thanks all the same." and with a last look at Blanche he disappeared into the nearest shop.

"Great kid, Sam. Shall I ask him to be our best man?"

Blanche didn't answer.

...

"This won't do, our Blanche. You just can't tell the lad you aren't going to marry him without giving him a reason."

"I have given him a reason, Mam. I don't love him enough. There's nothing you can say that will change my mind."

"I know why you're doing this. It's because of Sam, isn't it?"

"You won't change my mind about him either, so save your breath. His Mam's alright now. You know that, you've been to see her."

"Yes, I have been to see her and she's still not right. There's no proof that she'll improve either. She might even have a relapse so you can forget this idea about marrying Sam Watson, my girl."

"You've got a hope. I'll never forget about Sam. But I can wait." Blanche tossed her head, "Another eighteen months and I'll be twenty-one. Then you won't be able to stop me."

These arguments had been going on ever since Amy came back from the clinic and the fact that Blanche had now given Mark his ring back had sparked another row. That episode too had been another trial for Blanche.

"Why?" Mark had asked, "What have I done?"

"Nothing, Mark. I'm sorry but I just don't love you enough to marry you."

Mark gave her a questioning look, a hurt look, trying to come to terms with this rejection, then he said, "You told me you loved me, Blanche, why have you changed your mind? Is there someone else? No, there can't be," he answered his own question, "I'd have known if you were seeing somebody else. I just don't understand…" his voice trailed away in misery.

Blanche put her hand on his arm, "It's pointless trying to understand, Mark, and I'm sorry to hurt you like this but it's no use getting married and then finding we've made a mistake."

Mark rubbed his chin, "We…I had such plans for us, love."

"Yes, I know," Blanche said gently, "and I'm sorry."

He looked at the ring that lay in the palm of his hand. "What am I going to do with this? You'd better keep it, Blanche."

"No, Mark, I couldn't do that. You'll find some one else to wear it." there were tears in her eyes when she said, "I'm very fond of you, you know that, but it isn't enough to base a marriage on, really it isn't."

"Well, that's it then, is it?" Mark's question came through tight lips, "I'll always love you, Blanche. If you change your mind I'll be waiting."

"Please, Mark," Blanche was crying openly now.

Mark put his arms around her "Don't, love. It's alright. Don't cry."

That had been yesterday and today she faced her mother's wrath.

"...and you'll be out of here sharpish if you do, my girl." was Hilda's answer to Blanche's threat.

"Suits me," and Blanche flounced off with her nose in the air.

She'd broken off her engagement to Mark. She'd told her mother she was going to marry Sam, now all she had to do was tell him.

"There's a call for you Mr Watson," the telephone operator told him when he picked up the receiver on his desk.

"Yes?" Sam used his most business-like voice.

"It's me."

"Blanche?"

"I want to talk to you, Sam. Can you meet me tonight?"

"I suppose so. What's it about?"

"I'll tell you when I see you. We'll meet outside the Town Hall. OK?"

"I can't make it till eight."

"That's fine. Eight o'clock then. Bye, Sam."

Sam looked at the receiver for a while after he'd heard the click at the other end, wondering what she was up to now. She had said, '*I* want to talk to you' not '*we*' so it didn't include Mark. Sam put the telephone back on its cradle and tried to carry on with his work but he couldn't concentrate. Eventually he threw down his pen and decided he might as well get some lunch. He'd book a table at Toni's for tonight while he was out.

All afternoon he could think of no one but Blanche. He gazed out of his office window but all he saw was Blanche's face. "Blanche. Oh! Blanche," he said aloud. Why did she affect him this way and why did she have to turn up now just when he was coming to terms with the fact that she was marrying his best friend?

"Perhaps she's going to ask you to be best man at her wedding." Roger suggested when Sam told him about the 'phone call. It was a tongue in cheek answer to Sam's question of "I wonder what she wants?"

"You're joking."

"Yes, I am."

"Anyway, Mark would ask me, not Blanche."

"You'll have to wait to find out tonight, won't you?"

Roger had never had much time for Blanche and he prayed now that Sam wasn't going to get involved with her again. He realised there was nothing he could do about it if Sam did but the thought made Roger shudder. Sam was too good for her. Roger's opinion of Blanche was that she was a nasty piece of work. He had never forgiven her for what she'd done to Sam when they were youngsters and he saw no reason to change his mind about her now. All he could do, like Sam, was wait and see.

"You're looking very beautiful tonight, Blanche," Sam whispered as they were shown to their table.

"Thank you, Sam," and she looked at him from under those long lashes of hers, well aware of the effect it had on him.

For a while they sat scanning the menu then when they had ordered their meal and were left alone Sam asked, "Well, what's this all about?"

Blanche took a deep breath before she answered, "I've broken off my engagement to Mark."

Sam stared at her goggle-eyed, "You've what? Why?"

"Because I love you."

Sam gasped. He was finding it difficult to take this in.

"You do love me, don't you, Sam?"

Sam's throat was tight. "You know I do."

"I told Mam we were going to be married when I was twenty-one."

Sam swallowed hard. This was all too sudden and he told her so.

"No it isn't. Not for me it isn't."

"But you were going to marry Mark. I thought…"

"I'm fond of him, yes. If it hadn't been for you I would have married him but when I saw you that day in town I knew I couldn't go through with it. I do love you, Sam. Will you promise we'll be married when I'm twenty-one?"

"Blanche! Blanche!" Sam was laughing now, "Of course I will."

The waiter arrived with their meal.

"Congratulate me Toni. Blanche has just proposed."

"Why, Sam! That calls for a celebration," and he snapped his fingers at the wine waiter. "Alfredo, champagne for the lady and gentleman." then to Sam, "On the house. With our compliments."

"That's very generous of you, Toni. Thank you."

...

"So," Roger's disappointment was difficult to hide, "you've got your wish at last. Congratulations, Sam."

"Come on, Dad, be happy for me. I love her."

Roger decided to keep his opinions to himself. "Yes, of course, Sam. I know you love her and I want you to be happy." was all he could think of to say. He couldn't deny that Sam was happy these days, happier than he'd ever seen him. Maybe, he reasoned, the woman had changed. Maybe that spoilt brat of those early years had grown into a woman as kind and as gentle as she was lovely, for Roger had to admit that Blanche was lovely. It was what went on in that young woman's head that worried him. He prayed that Sam wouldn't be hurt again.

It was at breakfast some weeks later that Sam brought up his idea of taking Blanche to Spain. "Dad, I thought, if it's OK by you that is, I'd take some time off work and give her this holiday as an early birthday present. I had in mind to buy the engagement ring in Spain too. D'you think she'd like that?"

"I'm sure she would, Sam, but you'd better give her time to get some things together. Don't leave it until the last minute or you'll be in trouble. You know what women are."

There was trouble anyway for Sam. Thinking she would be pleased he gave her the plane tickets for their trip.

"What's this?" she asked, opening the envelope.

"I thought we might have a holiday . You'd enjoy a week in Spain, wouldn't you?"

Sam was smiling. Blanche wasn't. Blanche wanted -

had expected, an engagement ring and she was bitterly disappointed. After Sam had told her this morning over the 'phone that he had a surprise for her, she thought he'd bought a ring. She had told all her friends at work that she was getting engaged. How was she going to explain the fact that she had no ring? This really was too bad. He'd obviously spent the money on these stupid plane tickets.

"Spain?" she spat.

"Don't you want to go, Blanche?"

"I suppose. Now that you've bought the tickets."

"What's eating you now?" he realised she was spoiling for a row. "Something upset you, has it?"

She ignored his question. Instead, knowing it would annoy him she said, "I saw Mark today."

"What did he say? Did you tell him we were getting engaged?"

"No, because we're not, are we?"

Sam was beginning to get the message but he ignored her jibe. Instead he asked, "But you told him about us, didn't you?"

"No. Why should I?"

"You mean he doesn't know? When you broke off your engagement didn't you explain why?"

"No, I didn't."

"Don't you think that was a bit underhand? What will he think when he finds out? I think Mark deserves better than that, Blanche. He's a nice chap."

"You think! You think! Well you can think what you like. It's nothing to do with him what we're going to do."

Sam tried to placate her. "I'm just saying…"

"If I'd told him about you and me I'd have had to

explain why my Mam was against us getting married. I've no intention of telling him all our family business and neither will you."

"I wasn't… "

"…and if you think more about his feelings then you do about mine then perhaps I've made a mistake. Perhaps I should have stayed engaged to Mark. At least he gave me a ring to prove he loved me. Anyway, you go to Spain. Get yourself a Spanish bird. See if I care."

"Oh! Blanche, do shut up." Sam was weary of this argument, "You do talk some drivel."

"Drivel! I'll show you whether I'm talking drivel or not. You can keep your plane tickets." and she threw the envelope down on the path in front of him. "As far as I'm concerned that's it. We're through."

Sam was losing his temper now - not a thing he did very often. He was used to these outbursts, but she'd pushed him too far this time. "Do what you like you bad-tempered bitch. See if I care. I was going to get you a ring when we got to Spain but this has saved me a fortune. I'm glad we're finished because I don't want to end up with a shrew like you. You're just like your mother."

"Ugh!" was Blanche's reply as she turned and walked stiffly away, aware that he was watching.

Sam bent and picked up the envelope then he stood for a while before he too walked away. What a stupid thing to quarrel about, was his uppermost thought but she'd come round. She always did.

Blanche reached the corner of the street and for an instant she turned to see where he was. He'd gone. It had never occurred to her that he wouldn't come after her and say, 'Oh, come on, Blanche. What are we fighting about?' To find he'd gone was a shock. Surely he knew she didn't mean the things she'd said. Sam knew her better than anyone. He knew he only had to put his arms around her and say 'I love you, darling,' and everything would be alright. Had he really taken her seriously especially now, knowing what they knew, knowing all the happiness that was in store? She knew she'd gone too far when he'd said she was like her mother but Blanche could never back down at times like this. What a fool she was. Her mother's constant bickering had really got to her these days so that she snapped at everyone but she knew she had no reason to go for Sam the way she had. Tears wet her cheeks. She might have known Sam would buy her a ring, and anyway what did a ring matter. They loved each other. Well they had. Now she had lost him. She'd lost everything, everyone. She wished she was dead.

It took her only until she got home for her resolve to harden. She wasn't going to be the first to climb down. Sam would come round. He always did.

...

Sam went straight to his room when he got home, thankful that Roger was entertaining one of his lady friends and he didn't have to explain why he was back so soon from his date with Blanche.

He sat by the window hunched up in his misery. Why, he asked himself, had they had such a stupid row? But he knew why. Blanche was edgy, especially now, and more so when she'd had a taste of her mother's venom. Sam himself had been on edge waiting for the onslaught he expected from Hilda after her threats to take out a Court Order against him but it hadn't come. Not yet. What Sam didn't know was that Hilda had already been to see a solicitor whose advice had been to leave it alone. 'Your daughter is almost twenty years old,' the man had told her, 'so it's unlikely any action will be taken at this stage. Of course, if you insist I will put the procedure in motion' He had charged Hilda forty pounds for the privilege of this advice. What, she wondered would it cost her if she instructed him to proceed. So she had decided to drop the idea and deal with the problem in her own way. The sooner Blanche got away from the woman, Sam thought, the better it would be for them both. Her twenty-first birthday wasn't far away now and they had already been to look at some houses, one of which they particularly liked.

Thinking of their plans for the future lightened Sam's mood. The past few months had been very happy ones for them both. He thought back to the first time they had walked in the park. Blanche had said, "I haven't been here since that horrible man attacked me. It's all so different now, more open and…"

She was interrupted when Sam gasped, "They've cut down the willow tree." his face showed the dismay he felt, though why he should feel so bad about it he couldn't have said.

They stood close together where the tree had once spread its branches, the grass growing high around the stump - all that was left of his hideaway. The death of his willow seemed like an omen to Sam. He felt a shudder run through him, a shudder that Blanche felt as she clung to his arm. She bent down,

"It's not dead. There's a shoot coming up from the roots, a young willow, Sam. Look, love. It's only a tiny shoot now but it'll grow - grow fast, you'll see."

Sam nodded. Yes, another willow would grow from the roots of his old friend. He had to take comfort from that.

As they strolled along the path they looked for the spot where they had faced their ordeal all those years ago but the place was so changed it was impossible to be sure just where it had all happened. Slowly they walked on, their arms around each other, until they came to the river again and there the bank dipped steeply, making a shady hollow. They stopped. Sam kissed her. Gently she drew him down into the long grass and there, for the first time, they made love.

The weeks that followed were heady, glorious weeks. Sam smiled at the memory. They'd loved, they'd laughed, they'd made plans. Oh! what plans they'd made.

"We have to find a place of our own. I know it will be a while before we can be married but in the meantime we can collect what things we'll need and," Sam pulled her close to him, "it'll be somewhere to go when we want to be on our own."

Blanche had kissed him, "You're wonderful," she said. And he felt wonderful.

The following day Blanche had arrived with a pile of leaflets from the Estate Agent and together they sifted through the list, discarding the houses that were too big, too expensive, too whatever else they disliked about the property.

"How about this one?" Blanche wafted the sheet of paper under Sam's nose.

Sam read the blurb on the leaflet and rubbed his chin, "It's cheaper than the others but it's still too much."

"But it says it's in need of modernisation. That means it wants a bit of work doing to it. We could do a lot ourselves, Sam. I don't mind decorating, and we can try to get them to bring the price down."

"It's worth a try, I suppose. We've nothing to lose by asking, have we?"

It was a modest semi, in a modest avenue just off the main street, and according to the Estate Agent, at a modest price. Mr Pluckley told them that the old lady who had lived there had rather neglected the place. That, according to their guide, was the reason for the modest price, 'But' he added, when he saw the look of disgust on Blanche's face, "I feel sure the family will be open to any offers. The house has been on the market for some months now and the family want to sell as quickly as possible."

"You mean they're anxious to get their hands on the old woman's money." Blanche said.

"Well…yes. You could put it like that," said the embarrassed Mr Pluckley.

The outside of the house was unprepossessing to say the least. The garden was overgrown, the paint-work was peeling and one of the windows was broken. Inside the decor was dated. The living room walls were covered in a floral paper, faded, apart from the patches of bright colour where pictures had once hung. The dining room walls were papered in a Regency striped design, scuffed and stained where the table had stood against the wall. In the kitchen Blanche's look of disgust at the state of the sink and the grease-covered mottled grey cooker, wasn't lost on the Estate Agent.

"It certainly could do with a bit of a clean up," he told them.

"More than a bit," Blanche opened the cupboard doors on the kitchen cabinet and ran her finger through the dust.

"Yes, well.." he cleared his throat by way of apology, "shall we have a look upstairs ?"

Here again the walls were covered in floral wallpaper - big red hydrangeas covered the walls in the front bedroom, while the other bedroom was decorated with little pink roses. "Yuk." was Blanche's comment.

The bathroom's black and white tiles came only half way up the walls, the wall above painted pink The bath itself was a huge affair in white enamel, definitely the worse for wear, while the wash basin was cracked and the lavatory badly stained.

"And you're asking all that for it?" Sam said. Naming the sum printed on the leaflet.

"It's got potential."

"You're right but it's going to cost a fortune to reach that potential, don't you agree?"

"I suppose it will cost quite a bit, but the building itself is sound. There's no damp, as you can see, and the roof is in good condition." Blanche and Sam looked at him expectantly so he went on, "I'm sure the vendors would consider any reasonable offer, as I said."

"What do you consider a reasonable offer?" Blanche asked.

The man stated a price. Blanche laughed.

"Well, why not make an offer and see what the vendors

say? How's that?"

"Give us a day or two to think about it and we'll let you know."

Mr Pluckley's training came to the fore now. "I shouldn't leave it too long. At this price it will soon be snapped up."

"Then we'll find something else," Blanche retorted.

Sam smiled at the memory of that day. When they left the Estate Agent they each voiced their own ideas about what could be done to the house.

"That back room would look smashing with the walls done in pale lilac with darker curtains in the same colour at the window." was Blanches idea.

"I see it with a stronger colour, myself." Sam said

And so in their imagination they redecorated the whole house.

The following week they had made, to them, what seemed a ridiculously low offer and to their surprise it was accepted. Now they had to get a mortgage. It had all been so exciting until today. Until they'd had this silly quarrel. Sam sighed. They'd quarrelled before. It wouldn't last but he had to know if she was going to Spain with him or not, and soon.

CHAPTER 16

Sam waited for Blanche's call all week. It didn't come. Time was running out and with a sigh he realised he would have to be the one to break the deadlock.

"Bloody women!" he muttered to himself, "Why do I bother with 'em?"

He picked up the telephone then put it down again. Suppose it was Hilda who answered. Sam steeled himself against that possibility as he picked up the 'phone again and dialled, fervently hoping it would be anyone but his Aunt. He was out of luck.

"Hello!" Hilda's voice rattled his eardrums.

"Hilda," he sounded disappointed, even to his own ears, "How are you?"

"Oh! It's you, is it? What d'you want?"

Sam knew before he asked what the answer would be, "I want to speak to Blanche."

"She's not in," Hilda's voice was flat and unfriendly. She was lying. He knew it. "She's out with Mark," she added. This he realised was designed to annoy him but before he could make any reply the 'phone went dead.

Blanche, like Sam. had waited all week for his call. Each time the 'phone rang she had been there to answer it but today she had been too late, her mother had got there first.

With her back to Blanche, Hilda said, "Sorry, you've got the wrong number." knowing that Blanche stood behind her. Blanche's eyes narrowed. The back of her mother's neck was bright red, a sure sign that she was being devious.

"That was Sam, wasn't it?"

"So what if it was? I won't have him 'phoning you. You know how I feel and if I can stop you seeing him, I will."

"Yes, and I've told you you'll never do that. And I'll tell you something else. I'm going to Spain with him next week and there's nothing you can do about it."

Tempers rose and so did their voices. Hilda screamed, "We'll see about that, madam."

That was the moment Dave appeared in the kitchen doorway. Behind him stood Paul.

"Do you realise," Dave's voice was low and menacing. "that the whole street is out there listening to you two?"

"…and you've woken the baby." Paul chimed in, his face white with anger. "Eunice is too scared to come down for the baby's bottle. I'm fed up with all this rowing. The sooner we can get out of this house the better. I'd sooner live in Joe's shed than stay here." and with that he charged up the stairs two at a time, slamming the bedroom door behind him.

Dave moved further into the hall. He was furious and it showed.

"I'll tell you now, the pair of you, I'm sick to death of coming home to scenes like this. If she," and he inclined his head towards his daughter, "wants to go off with Sam, then let her. The sooner she's out of this house the better, and I'll tell you something else, if I come home to another row like this I'll pack my bags and go, along with our

Paul."

The two women stared at him in open-mouthed silence. They had never seen Dave so angry. He had always been so quiet and easy going. This outburst shocked them both.

Hilda, her face still red from her quarrel with Blanche got even redder at the thought of the neighbours hearing what had been said. Now she whispered, "Dave! You wouldn't leave me."

"Wouldn't I? Just try me, woman," and he stalked back into the kitchen, a look of disgust on his face.

Hilda followed, "I'm sorry, Dave. I didn't realise. I didn't think..."

But the look he gave silenced her, she sat down and, putting her elbows on the table, burst into tears.

The atmosphere in the Watson household was frosty to say the least, after this episode. The only exchanges were stilted remarks made between sullen silences. Paul and Dave still furious. Blanche sullen. Hilda contrite - at least as far as her husband and Paul were concerned.

Blanche's sullen mood though, was mainly due to the fact that she couldn't contact Sam. She tried to ring him at home and at work but without success. She went round to The Garth, only to find there was no one at home. It was Paul who eventually carried Sam's message to her.

"Sam 'phoned me at work," he told her grudgingly. "He's had to go with Roger to Manchester. Some meeting or other. He says he'll be there all week but he'll meet you at the airport, OK? I told him you were still going to Spain with him. Is that right or have you changed your mind again?"

Blanche nodded. "...and don't tell anybody I've given

you that message, our Blanche. I've done it for Sam, not you. Eunice says we have to keep out of it and she's right."

"I won't say anything, Paul, I promise."

"How are you going to get there?"

"Well, I thought you…"

"NO. I told you. I'm not getting involved."

"I'll get a taxi then."

"That'll cost you."

"What's the alternative. I can't carry all my luggage across Manchester, can I?"

…

Blanche looked again at her watch. The taxi was late. She had waited until her mother went to the shops before she called the taxi office. The man at the other end of the 'phone said, "We'll be there in ten minutes. That was twenty minutes ago. Another ten minutes went by before the cab drew up outside the gate. Fumbling with her luggage Blanche made for the door that the driver held open.

"Manchester Airport. Is that right?" he asked.

Blanche glared at him, "And don't mess about. I have a plane to catch."

The driver, a young man, not much older than Blanche, gave her a cheeky grin. "Hold on to your…"

"Don't say it," Blanche snapped.

"I was going to say, hat."

Expertly he negotiated the traffic through the town while Blanche sat fuming in the back seat. Over the moors he drove at a furious rate, throwing his passenger from side to side as the car swung round the bends in the road. It was when they reached the built-up area that they hit the traffic and had to slow to a crawl

Blanche looked at the time on her watch, “Can’t you go any faster?”

“Would you like to try?”

“I’ll miss my plane.”

“You should have started earlier.”

“You’re right. Half-an-hour earlier if you’d arrived on time.”

The car in front jerked into action. “Here we go,” and the driver put his foot down on the accelerator passing half-a-dozen cars in the process then, without warning a car pulled out in front of them. The taxi driver swore and swerved but it was too late. Metal screamed on metal. Blanche screamed in unison as her head hit the back of the seat in front, then the impact threw her against the door, knocking the breath out of her. Through a haze she heard the raised voices of both drivers, each accusing the other of causing the accident. Neither had any thought for the passenger in the back of the taxi. Dazedly Blanche tried once more to see what time it was, “I have to get to the airport,” she wailed but no one took any notice.

Minutes later the police arrived followed shortly after by the ambulance.

“Where are you hurt, miss?” the ambulance man felt her pulse and examined the bump on her forehead.

“I’m not. I’m alright.” the man could see she was shaking but it was as much from anger as from shock.

“Come on,” gently he helped her out of the damaged car, “let’s get you to hospital.”

“No, I can’t,” Blanche tried to resist, “Please, get me to the airport,” but all her efforts and pleas were ignored.

Fifteen minutes later she found herself in the Casualty Department of a hospital. But which hospital? Someone asked her for her name and address. She told them, then asked "Where am I?" a question the nurse took to be confusion.

"You'll be alright, love," the nurse assured her after they'd examined her bumps and bruises, "Nothing broken. We've 'phoned your parents and you can go home as soon as they come for you."

Blanche tried to protest but the woman rustled out of the cubicle without even acknowledging that she had heard. Her head ached, her shoulder was sore. Blanche lay back on the trolley and wept. This was a disaster. Sam would think she was still mad at him. He'd never speak to her again, ever.

How are you feeling now?" the nurse bent over her and took her pulse once more. Blanche opened her eyes and wondered how long she'd been there. "Your brother's come to take you home. Do you feel well enough to travel?" the nurse didn't wait for an answer but helped Blanche to her feet. Paul poked his head round the curtain, "Are you hurt?" he asked, and when she shook her head, "You're a menace, d'you realise that? A bloody menace. Come on." and he helped her out of the cubicle.

"Alright, so I'm a menace, but I have to tell Sam what's happened."

"And how do you propose to do that, then?" Paul's voice held more than a note of sarcasm.

"I'm going to 'phone the airport, what else. Have you any change?" Blanche held out her hand and with a sigh of resignation Paul emptied his pockets of the coins he had.

"He'll have gone by now. They'll have boarded the plane ages ago."

But Blanche's watch told her she still had time. "I'm going to try, anyway."

Waiting for the 'phone to be answered stretched her already taut nerves almost to screaming pitch so when finally, a voice announced she was through, she explained in sharp words that she needed to get a message to one of the passengers on Flight 147 to Spain.

"I'll put you through to the Departure Lounge," the voice said.

Another wait. Blanche tapped her fingernails on the telephone directory.

"Departure Lounge," she heard at last.

"I want to get an urgent message to Sam Watson. He's a passenger on Flight 147 to Spain."

"I'm sorry. The passengers are already boarding the plane."

"Please! It's urgent.Desperately urgent."

Something in Blanche's voice must have touched a cord, the receptionist said, "Well, I'll try. What's the message?"

"Tell him it's from Blanche and that I've had an accident. No don't tell him that, he'll worry. Say that I've had trouble getting to the airport and that I'll join him in Spain as soon as I can. Tell him I love him, will you? Please, please make sure he gets my message."

"I'll do my best, I promise," the voice said and Blanche had to be content with that.

' ' '

Sam searched the faces of the passengers as they filed

onto the plane. No Blanche. Why? Paul had definitely said she was coming. Oh! Blanche, his heart cried out for her. This was to have been such a wonderful holiday. Their engagement. Their special secret. He'd felt sure she would come. Why hadn't she come? Sam turned away, despairing, as the last passenger came on board. He decided right then to catch the next flight back. A touch on his shoulder made him turn quickly in his seat, hopeful that after all Blanche was here, but it was the Stewardess.

"There's a message for you, Mr Watson," and she put the note in his hand.

Clumsily he opened the folded paper and as he read it a whole gamut of emotions swept over him. Joy, that she said she loved him, disappointment, that she wouldn't be travelling with him, and hope when he read that she would be joining him later. He tucked the note in his pocket, smiled his thanks at the Stewardess and resigned himself to a lonely flight but a holiday to look forward to. Yes, Sam was happy.

CHAPTER 17

Blanche lay on the settee in the front room fussed over by Hilda, all differences between them forgotten, although her mother couldn't resist saying,

"If you'd done as you were told this wouldn't have happened, would it?"

Blanche felt too miserable to reply. She slept. It was the voice of the newsreader that woke her.

"What was that, Dad?" she asked, wide awake now.

Her father sat with his elbows on his knees, hands clasped in front of him. "Some plane or other crashed."

"What plane? Where from? Where to?"

"Manchester, they said. Going to Spain."

"What was the flight number, d'you remember?" Blanche had heard but she wanted confirmation. She was sure the announcer said Flight 147, or was it 714? There'd been a telephone number to ring too, what was it? She got up too quickly. Her head knocked and the room swam dizzily round her. She hung on to the back of her father's chair for a moment but she hadn't time to hang about. She had to find out, had to know if it was Sam's flight. Blanche steadied herself then slowly she made her way into the hall.

The telephone on Roger's desk rank twice. He glared at it. It continued to ring. He cursed and picked up the receiver. A voice said, "It's Blanche." before she could say anymore he yelled. "Get off this line. I'm waiting for an urgent call." and he slammed down the receiver.

Panic took hold of her. He'd said he was waiting for an urgent call. That could only mean he was waiting for news of Sam. She had to get round there.

"I'm going to see Sam's Dad," she announced to her father.

"What are you going there for?"

"That plane. It was the one Sam was on. The one I should have been on."

"Oh! Lord, Oh, No." was all Dave could say.

Blanche grabbed her coat and went out through the front door, closing it behind her with a bang.

"Where's our Blanche going?" Hilda came into the room with a tea towel in her hands.

"She's gone round to Roger Wilmott's. That plane Sam was on has crashed."

"Oh!" was Hilda's only comment.

"Oh! Is that all you can say? Oh! Sam could be hurt. He could be dead."

"What d'you want me to say. Of course I don't want anything to happen to Sam but…"

"But it would save you a lot of trouble if he was, wouldn't it? You didn't talk like that when he saved our Blanche from being raped, did you?"

Things had never been the same in the Watson household since Dave's threat to leave. Since then he had taken on a more masterful role and Hilda knew better than to argue.

…

Roger heard the ring of the doorbell. "Go away," he growled. This was no time for visitors. He wanted to be alone. But the noise was persistent. He swore and went to open the door. It was Blanche who stood there.

"I thought you were going with Sam?"

"I... I...was but I had an accident." she pointed to the bruise on her forehead.

Roger still barred the way.

"I've come to see if you've heard anything about Sam - about the crash?" Her face was pale, her eyes bright with unshed tears. "Please. Tell me if you have."

"Better come in," Roger relented his decision to keep her out but there was no pity in his voice. He felt none for this girl. If Sam was hurt it was her fault. Sam had gone to Spain for her sake. She should have been with him.

Blanche echoed his thoughts. "I should have been with him. I should have been there. Oh! Sam. Sam," she sobbed. "I heard the news on the television but I didn't get the 'phone number. I was hoping you had."

"You'd better sit down. Yes, I rung but there's no news yet. They said they'd ring me back."

Blanche sat with her head bowed. "I know you don't like me very much but I want you to know that I do love Sam." Roger sat down in the chair opposite her and she could see from his expression that he wasn't impressed. "I've done some rotten things to him, I know. I thought I hated him but after that incident in the park all that changed. Sam understands that and he understands me. He's the only one who does. He knows I don't mean half the things I say when I'm angry but when we are married things'll be different. He knows I need to get away from Mam. We've got such plans, Mr Wilmott. Did Sam tell you we've been looking at a house?" Blanche didn't wait for an answer, "It's quite near the hospital and we thought, now that Aunty Amy's so much better, she could come and visit us when we get settled in. Did you know that she helps out on the ward these days? The new Matron calls her 'my right-hand woman'. "

Blanche's nervous chatter went on and on. Roger had seen her like this before just after their ordeal in the park. He let her rattle on, his thoughts on Sam. Roger was remembering the early days when he and Sam were getting to know one another, remembering how grown up Sam had tried to appear that first time he'd taken him to Toni's restaurant. He was remembering too that first summer. He'd told Sam he would take him anywhere he wanted to go - football matches, cricket matches - but Sam's choice had surprised him.

"Can we go to Jodrell Bank to see the telescope?" he'd asked. He'd also asked to go to the aerodrome to see the planes take off. But they'd done better than that. Roger smiled to himself now at that memory. Sam had been thrilled when they took a trip - a very short trip it was - in a plane. Yes that had been a wonderful year. Fancy remembering that just now when Sam might be.... No he couldn't let himself think that way. Blanche was still talking. Roger only half listened until he caught the words, "....and she was so happy when we told her about the ba... that we were getting married" Roger looked up sharply at this,

"You were going to say something about a baby." he accused. "You're going to have a baby. Sam's baby."

Blanche's incessant chatter ceased. Suddenly she looked frightened, "Don't tell Mam, please. When Sam comes back and we're married it won't matter. She can't do anything about it then, can she?"

"What does Sam say about it?"

"He's thrilled, like I am, but I haven't seen the doctor yet so I can't be absolutely sure."

Roger gave her a searching look. So, she was having Sam's child. His grandchild. It had to be a boy - young Sam. Yes, they'd call him Sam like his father. He'd have to put up with this woman, he supposed, because he wasn't going to miss out on this baby. He said it aloud now, "Sam's baby. Sam's son. My grandson." and it gave him a warm glow inside.

The 'phone rang. The shrill of it brought him back to reality with a start. He looked at it where it stood on the desk. It seemed to bounce with the urgency of its message but Roger made no effort to answer it. He was afraid of what that message might be.

"The 'phone," Blanche said impatiently, wanting to snatch it from its cradle.

Slowly, deliberately Roger picked it up and put it to his ear. "Wilmott," he said.

Blanche saw the colour drain from his face. She knew before he spoke what that message was.

As if hypnotised he put the receiver down turning bleak eyes to her, "Sam's dead," he told her, "They're all dead."

Blanche tried to stand up. She swayed and held on to the desk to stop herself from falling. The room whirled around her and a grey mist came up in front of her eyes. She fought it off. She mustn't faint, not here, not in front of Sam's father, he thought little enough of her as it was. But Roger saw her distress and putting out his hand to support her, gently sat her down again. He poured a drink and offered her the glass.

"Here, drink this, it'll steady you," and he filled another glass for himself.

For a long time they sat each with their own thoughts, then Blanche said, her voice hoarse with emotion, "It was the willow tree. They chopped it down, you know. When Sam saw what they'd done he was upset, very upset but I showed him the new shoot that was growing up from the old roots. I remember he smiled but it was such a sad smile. I think he realised it was an omen. That shoot was this baby," and Blanche held a hand to her stomach. "It's like Sam being born again."

Roger's throat was too tight to say anything. He just took hold of her other hand and held it between his own.